J.A. K

FOREVER FATED

novum ◢ pro

This book is also available as e-book.

www.novum-publishing.co.uk

© 2022 novum publishing

ISBN 978-3-99131-007-5
Editing: Ashleigh Brassfield, DipEdit
Cover photos:
Vladimirs Poplavskis, Chernetskaya, Natthamon Yanasing | Dreamstime.com
Cover design, layout & typesetting: novum publishing

www.novum-publishing.co.uk

Climate neutral
Print product
ClimatePartner.com/16547-2201-1002

DEDICATION

To Lynne, Tony and the lads without whom this would not have been possible. Your input and patience was invaluable to me.

$\mathscr{Y}$

Lisa Mason was a petite brunette with sparkling blue eyes and a smile that illuminated the world. Always bullied by the girls at school, jealous of the attention she received, attracting the boys like moths to a flame with her easy manner, pretty face and long, thick, naturally corkscrewed locks, Lisa was blissfully oblivious of this fact, her head being filled with all things equine. She could never understand why her own sex saw her as such a threat, a theme that would sadly follow her throughout her life. In order to escape a mother who saw her as less than her brothers, always leaving her until last in her consideration in all things, Lisa met and hastily married John Metcalf, a kind youth, if a little odd, and at the age of 18 their first child was born, a baby girl called Lynette. Lisa was the driving force in the relationship, wanting to buy their first home. Her love of horses had become an obsession and she quickly realised that to do both she would have to work hard to fund her dreams. She worked at many jobs, her favourite being at the livery stables, where she learned her trade. She quickly gained the reputation of being an accomplished horsewoman, breaking and schooling young horses, gaining her Horse Master's degree in double-time. A friend for whom she had schooled a pony had told her that there would be a cleaning job coming up for grabs, as the woman who had it was leaving because of family difficulties, and that she would put her name forward to take over her duties.

As Lisa walked down the path of the neat little cottage, the middle of a trio nestled at the end of a wooded lane, she was taken by the heady perfume of honeysuckle. It climbed over the garden walls and surrounded the picture-perfect cottage, giving it an almost fairytale quality that made her feel instantly at ease. She had been given the key to the property by Jenny, the woman who had kept it in tip top order up until her husband's illness. Lisa entered the cottage and stood looking round at the neat, well-appointed rooms.

'Where to start ...' she mused. Just as she was scanning the invitingly comfortable rooms, the door opened and was filled by a broad pair of shoulders draped in an expensive three-piece suit. At six feet one inch tall, Gareth Edwards had short-cropped blond hair, strikingly vivid blue eyes and a clear tanned complexion, his chiselled features and jaw set in a business-like manner. The Armani suit he wore accentuated his muscular body and formidable arms. Lisa caught her breath at his appearance; he had taken her by surprise. 'Dear God, he is gorgeous,' she thought as he unfolded through the door into the room. Lisa had been told that he was a solicitor and that he had recently qualified. He introduced himself; his voice was deep, rich, strong, and impeccably spoken. He appeared a little aloof, very matter of fact and concise – a typical legal eagle.

He quickly explained to her what her duties were to be and that he would pay her the sum of five pounds per hour, a king's ransom to her. 'What a Godsend,' Lisa thought, elated. He left just as abruptly as he had arrived, leaving Lisa a little bewildered. 'He was very proper,' she thought, almost stuck up in the way he spoke, a far reach from her broad Lancashire twang.

As he climbed into his BMW outside the cottage his mind was in turmoil, heart pumping so fast against his ribcage it took his breath away. 'What the hell is wrong with you, man?' he spoke the words out loud, looking at his face in the vanity mirror, seeing the beads of sweat forming on his forehead. He had never had this reaction to a woman before; in fact, his total lack of interest in the opposite sex had many of his colleagues and friends assuming that he was gay, but none dared voice their opinion due to his volcanic temper. Those strangers who mistakenly chose to voice their opinions usually ended up in hospital.

He started the car and pulled away from the cottage, trying to concentrate on the road, although he could not shake the image of the slender brunette from his mind; her tight jeans with the T-shirt tucked in at her neat waist. She had a rear that he wanted to sink his teeth into, her corkscrew locks cascaded over her shoulders, now sporting blond highlights, and her chunky ankle boots gave her slim form an almost tomboyish appearance. He was taken by her beautiful, makeup-free, flawless skin and the fact that her eyes sparkled when she laughed, lighting the world. He had noticed that her eyes were gun metal blue with fine threads of green and hazel. Gareth thought her the most naturally attractive woman he had come across, yet he could not understand his reaction. He had never trusted women, a legacy from his past, yet he could find no excuse to ignore her. She was simply lovely and scary at the same time, making him uncomfortable with her easy chatty manner.

As time passed, Gareth found himself drawn to the house and made excuses at the office to go home. He would try to rush in and out, but she would ambush him and engage him in conversation, which made him feel like a rabbit caught in headlights; yet still he was drawn to her in a way that had him worried, almost running scared. He could not understand why or how he felt as he did about this woman, yet he craved her attention and for the first time in his life, at the age of 23, he felt stirrings of a sexual nature that were totally alien to him.

She started to care for him during his fleeting visits and would prepare a sandwich and drink for him, going beyond the brief of her duties. He found her easy manner endearing and soon warmed to her chatty, silly ways and the way she made him talk and laugh.

He was travelling home to see her for the first time this week, almost giddy with anticipation. He breathed in the warm honeysuckle scented air as he breezed down the path in the heat of the summer sun. He floated through the door to find her busy making lunch for him and humming some tune to herself.

'Hiya,' she beamed as he sauntered in, 'I've made you a sandwich and a drink.' He smiled at the view of her delectable rump and tiny waist and thanked her. As she turned to face him, he stopped mid stride.

'What on earth have you done?' he asked with a worried tone, wanting to take a closer look but still not confident enough to touch her.

'A stable door caught me when the wind blew it shut yesterday,' she replied, placing the cup and plate on the table.

He nodded and walked past her feeling uneasy. He washed his hands, and on his return, he said, 'Let's try that one again shall we? Are you going to tell me what happened to your face?'

She peered at him with the look of someone caught out in a lie. 'I told you, the wind –'

He interrupted her mid-sentence. 'There was no wind yesterday, it was a still summer's day, try again.'

She looked totally crestfallen. Her breath caught in her throat as she told him that John had been drunk and punched her during an argument. He felt the bile rise in this throat and his lips were white with the rage he was barley containing. Why did he feel so protective of this woman? How had she managed to get under his skin at all, let alone in such a short space of time? He was finding it increasingly more difficult to concentrate at work, images and thoughts of her flooding his every waking moment; hell, he was even dreaming about her now. He ate his sandwich and chatted to Lisa, well, mainly listened to her lilting happy chatter, transfixed by her laugh and her joy in life even though she bore the marks of violence on her lovely face. She was a pleasure to be around; she seemed to lift the weight from his world.

In the past he had found the need to install a camera in his home as some of his previous cleaning ladies, prior to Jenny, had proven to be less than trustworthy, going through his possessions and on one occasion actually stealing money from a dresser drawer in his bedroom. He had left it in place merely as a precaution, assuring himself that all was as it should be. He would check it fortnightly, as a rule, but since the advent of Lisa in his life he found that he was checking it more often, and not for the reasons the camera was intended, his need to see her becoming paramount. After a stressful day at the office, he would rush home, make a brew of green tea and settle down in front of the camera, rewinding the tape to where Lisa's form appeared. He smiled as he watched her singing along at the top of her voice to the music playing on the radio, dancing with the vacuum cleaner, and using the feather duster as a microphone. God, how he wanted her, yet past events haunted him, barring his way forward. He played the tape over and over watching avidly her every move. He was actually feeling guilty for having the camera in place and had the urge to tell her of its existence, but then he would have to forego the pleasure of watching Lisa dance her way round his home. Perhaps he would wait a little longer to tell her. Was he becoming a voyeur? Gareth quickly shook his head, dismissing the thought out of hand.

Lisa always believed that she had been put on this earth to help those in need. It didn't matter if they had two legs or four, she had a natural empathic ability that drew her to any being that was damaged by life, knowing instinctively when she needed to intervene.

She was working at the cottage, singing at the top of her voice when the door opened. She had prepared lunch for Gareth, as it had become part of her routine. In addition, she had also ironed shirts that she found in the washing basket. As she turned toward the door her heart sank; she immediately felt that all was not well with the man that faced her. His whole demeanour was one of defeat, not something that ever sat well or for long on his broad shoulders.

'Aw, what's wrong?' she said, startling him from his thoughts and taking a step forward, arms outstretched, to administer a healing hug. He immediately blocked her advance with the long reach of his arms. Looking at her lovely face he heard her say apologetically, 'Sorry, I've overstepped the mark,' holding her hands up and taking a step backwards. She could feel the heat in her cheeks.

It was at that moment, as he watched the blush spread over her cheeks, that Gareth took a leap of faith. Pulling her towards his chest, he kissed her forehead, his chin brushing the top of her head as he stooped to meet her, burying his head in the nape of her neck, and holding her tightly against his torso for what seemed like an age to Lisa. At that very moment he felt the exquisite pain of cupid's arrow pierce his heart as it thawed and melted. He had never felt a rush of emotion like this in his entire life; she had to be his one and only. They sat drinking the brew that Lisa prepared while he ate his lunch. He was becoming acutely aware of the discomfort from his growing erection that pressed solidly against his suit pants. She questioned the reason for his troubled expression. He found the whole experience exhausting; never before had he let another human being see his pain, yet here he sat having every word coaxed from him. He recounted having found out that his stepfather had sold the family legal practice for a pound on the day had he qualified to prevent Gareth from inheriting the firm. The man had hated him from the moment he discovered that he wasn't his child but the result of an affair that his wife had with a handsome local farmer. The loathsome man had made it his mission in life to punish the beautiful little blonde-haired boy for his wife's infidelity, subjecting him to a catalogue of abuse that spanned his early years and beyond. God only knew he dared not speak of the torture that he had suffered at the hands of his mother, which made his stepfather's pale in comparison, for fear of appearing less of a man. Perhaps one day, but until then he would bury that dark secret deep.

Lisa listened after pulling every last piece of confessional from his lips. She could see that he was drained by the effort of releasing the burden he felt and made a mental note to revisit the subject at the first available opportunity, knowing instinctively that there were depths and layers that needed peeling away but having no idea of the horror that she would eventually discover. Gareth climbed back in his car feeling as if he had just had a full work out. He was drained, yet felt lighter, easier in himself. He shook his head and thought, 'Dear God, what has that woman done to me?'

Lisa's home life was deteriorating, becoming increasingly more violent. John Metcalf proved to be an inadequate, jealous partner, turning to drink to drown the sickening feeling in the pit of his gut. He took to verbal abuse at first to make himself feel better, pulling Lisa down at every available opportunity, telling her no one would want her or ever look at her, that she was worth nothing. This became a weekly routine. He would go out, getting increasingly more wasted. The more he drank the more belligerent and violent he became; this often led to him taking a beating from the men at the places he frequented as he made clumsy drunken advances toward their women.

John was small in stature and a little sickly-looking, which only served to fuel his feelings of inadequacy. The rage that brewed inside him came from watching a long line of admirers that found Lisa 'A friendly, easy lass to talk to,' as they would say. One of her jobs of an evening was at the Withy Tree public house – the landlord Bob thought highly of Lisa as she drew in the male punters, filling his bar and his pockets. John's toxic put-downs caused Lisa to cover her form with baggy off-the-shoulder tops that draped loosely over her body, having the opposite effect to the one desired. The tops proved to be far more alluring to the male punters, which boosted Bob's profits, of course, serving also to bring wives and partners to the bar in order to see what the pull was to their increasingly absent menfolk. This usually culminated in the ejection of all parties concerned, in particular John, who invariably waded into the fray, escalating any problems that existed. Lisa was naïve enough to believe that the attention she received from the many male admirers that frequented the bar, engaging her in chit chat, was merely 'folks being friendly.' After all, John had told her how fat and ugly she was so many times she began to believe it to be true.

Arriving home from the night shift at the bar, John followed Lisa in, staggering drunkenly through the door. 'Give me the fucking car keys,' he barked, spitting the slurred words at her as he slumped against the wall.

'No way, look at the state of you, you are not fit to drive,' she replied. The rage exploded inside him and he lunged forward, grabbing her wrist as she closed her fist quickly around the keys to stop him taking them, which earned her a sickening blow to her face, cracking her eye socket. The keys bit hard into the soft flesh of her palm as he repeatedly smashed her clenched fist against the wall, busting her knuckles. All Lisa could think was 'Thank God that Lynette's at her grandparents,' as the pain tore through her hand. The exertion eventually proved too much for him, the effects of the alcohol he had consumed finally overwhelming him as he collapsed in a heap on the floor. Lisa strode over his prone body as it lay across the narrow entrance hall and climbed the stairs, dazed and bleeding, steadying herself on the handrail. She cleaned and treated her face and hand the best she could with what she had in house.

The following morning no amount of concealer could mask the damage to her eye socket, which had swollen to the extent that the eye had closed completely. It throbbed, her head ached, and her lip had been split during the struggle. 'God, I look like a train wreck,' she thought. As she came down the stairs John's crumpled heap lay where it had fallen the night before. She checked to see if he was breathing, then strode over him, leaving to turn the horses out and head for Honeysuckle Cottage. She was not prepared to answer any questions about her injuries that morning; most seemed satisfied that she had been injured whilst breaking a horse that proved a little awkward. She knew one person who would not be satisfied with her explanation, so did her best to avoid him.

As Gareth entered the kitchen, he called, 'Lisa, where are you?'

She was cleaning the bathroom. 'Won't be a moment,' she called, 'your early lunch isn't ready yet.'

He had rushed home early on the pretence that he needed papers for a case he was working on, needing to have a fix of his drug of choice. As she entered the kitchen, she saw him flinch, his beautiful perfect smile changing to an angry, troubled grimace. 'Another stable door, I presume,' he said, barely concealing the venom in his tone. She looked crestfallen and nodded sheepishly. 'This is not right, you know.' He was trying to soften his voice so as not to upset her with his reactions, but found it difficult to choke back the bile in the back of his throat. 'You shouldn't have to hide away from me or anyone else because you have taken a beating from that lowlife.'

Her embarrassment at his statement welled up and she snapped back, 'Well, it really is no one else's business, is it?' She knew that he was concerned and instantly regretted her barbed response. He turned to go back through the door, and she returned to her chores.

Moments later she heard a loud crack and the sound of splintering wood but did not witness the single punch that hit the door, splitting it in two and knocking it from its hinges. She ran as quickly as her aching legs would carry her only to see Gareth leaning with his hands on the garden wall, head down, breathing laboured as his anger took hold. He looked up to see Lisa astonished face peering at him through the space where the door used to be.

'Please forgive my outburst,' he said as he walked past her, back into the house, pausing to stroke her arm in reassurance. Picking up the phone he dialled the joiner. The man recognised Gareth's voice instantly, having worked for him previously, and listened as the tale unfolded of an incident that had occurred at Honeysuckle Cottage involving the property no longer being secure; Gareth said that he had been the incident and to attend as soon as possible to secure the premises.

Replacing the handset, he returned to Lisa, who had made them a piping hot brew of green tea, both in need of a break to regain their composure. The more he looked at the damage to her face and hand, the more he resolved to sort Metcalf out.

Lisa complained that her head ached, and her eye was becoming more painful. After much persuasion he convinced her that she should go to the A&E department of Preston Royal Infirmary, but only after the joiner had replaced the door. Gareth rang the office and told them he would be working from home for the rest of the day; he didn't intend to leave anything to chance, taking Lisa to the hospital. He stayed by her side steadying her as she walked guiding her through the corridors. The attending doctor informed them that the eye socket was in fact fractured, discharging Lisa on the understanding that she rest and took the painkillers that he prescribed. Gareth dropped Lisa home, making sure that she was comfortable. She breathed a sigh of relief to find that John was not longer at home.

That night as John Metcalf staggered home from his usual watering hole down the back streets of Preston, concentrating on his footing in the dim light, he didn't see the tall figure step from the shadows, a baseball cap pulled down to mask the face of a man whose teeth were clenched, jaw set and lips white with rage. Metcalf could barely remember the kick that smashed through his jaw, splattering blood over his face and choking his airways as he hit the hard cobbled stones, let alone the kicking that followed. His assailant growled with menace, close to his ear as he lay there bleeding: 'Touch her again and I will kill you.' The figure walked away from the scene of devastation he had inflicted. Heading towards the nearest phone box he dialled the emergency services, informing them to send an ambulance to where Metcalf's body lay.

The following morning the Royal contacted Lisa informing her that her husband was admitted with serious injuries in the early hours of that day. As she walked down the ward she could see John's limp prone body, curtain partially drawn round where he lay. 'Dear God,' she thought, 'he looks like he has been hit by a truck.' His features were swollen, bloody and distorted, both eyes puffy and closed. 'Retribution,' she thought, believing that his drunken antics had earned him yet another beating, yet this was far more serious than any that had gone before. She wondered who had been pissed enough to unleash such destruction on another; Joe Fraser could not have done a better job in ten rounds. He wasn't in the mood for talking and blanked Lisa's questions, ignoring her presence. After ten minutes of silence, she rose and went in search of a nurse to find out what she needed to know. The staff nurse told her that John was stable and would be kept in for 48 hours, as there were concerns that his kidneys had been damaged which warranted further investigation. Lisa left the hospital without returning to John's bedside, making her way to the carpark. She got into her car and headed to the first job of the day.

The cottage kitchen was clean and tidy – Gareth was ever organised. She gave the work surfaces a cursory wipe down and checked the washing basket for ironing. He had been so pleasantly surprised at the way she had ironed his shirts without tram lines on the sleeves that he included that task in her duties, upping her money to ten pounds as a result. Finishing that chore, she retrieved the vacuum cleaner from the cupboard under the stairs. Dragging it into the lounge, she bent, plugging the appliance in at the wall. As she straightened up, the sunlight that flooded that room glinted on three objects, catching her eye. On the table at the far end of the long plush settee the sun bounced off the metallic objects. Leaving the cleaner where it stood, she walked across the room to the table. There in plain sight were three handguns, carefully positioned on a cloth that draped the table, protecting its highly polished surface from the metal. Lisa had only ever seen guns like this in films and was taken aback to discover three sidearms laying out in full view. She was afraid to handle them for fear of setting one off by mistake, yet curiosity getting the better of her she scanned them closely.

Deep in thought, she hadn't heard the door open or Gareth's hasty entrance. He had been at the office, unable to concentrate, Lisa flooding his every waking thought. What would she be doing now ... He looked at his watch; she would be cleaning up a storm. He froze.

'Oh dear god,' he exclaimed out loud, and grabbed his car keys. Racing to his car, he sped off toward the cottage. On his arrival he composed himself as he walked through the lounge door, taking in the scenario that faced him.

'I am so sorry, Lisa, I forgot to lock them away after I cleaned them last evening. I brought them home from the gun club to inspect them and forgot about them.'

Lisa smiled, totally at ease with the explanation he proffered, being blissfully ignorant of the fact that sidearms were illegal in the United Kingdom unless kept under lock and key at a licensed gun club, each carrying a five-year prison sentence for possession. Gareth quickly removed the Smith & Wesson, Glock, and Colt from the table, taking them into his bedroom and placing them in the metal gun case that he kept at the back of his wardrobe. 'Careless,' he muttered under his breath, 'very careless.'

They sat at the table, chatting about horses, a common interest although he had no formal training in equitation. He found Lisa's passion infectious, delighting in her antics and the way she sparkled when she spoke. 'Mine,' he thought to himself, 'I have to have her.'

John Metcalf's moods had become increasingly unstable, dropping him to the depths of despair, his only solace found at the bottom of a bottle. His drinking was out of control, spilling over into his workplace and eventually culminating in his dismissal. Lisa suddenly found herself the only breadwinner in the family, the monies she earned having to keep them plus the horses that she had acquired. She made sure that little Lynette, John, and the horses were fed, often going without nourishment herself as John showed little inclination towards pulling himself out of his malaise.

Gareth arrived home for lunch, the happiest time of his day, Lisa greeting him with a beaming smile that warmed his world. Placing his lunch before him, she asked, 'Do you mind if I make a sandwich for myself?'

'Of course not, please help yourself.' He was puzzled and a little concerned.

'You can dock it from my wages,' she offered, but he frowned at the thought, shaking his head. As his eyes wandered over her body, luxuriating in the feast before them, he noted that she had dropped weight.

'Is everything ok with you, Lisa?' he enquired.

'I haven't eaten in three days,' she said under her breath, a little ashamed.

'Why on earth not?' His alarm was obvious at the revelation. She explained as they ate lunch together that she was now the only wage earner in the family and the circumstances that had brought about the situation. Finishing lunch, she removed the cups and plates to the sink. As she turned, the heat from the proximity of Gareth's body hit her as he pulled her into his arms. Cupping her face with his hands he kissed her as she had never been kissed before, tasting her lips, nipping, sucking, relishing every last morsel. She melted into his body, responding to his every move. He suddenly realized that this was fast approaching the point of no return for him, as Lisa's body yielded to his touch. He felt that he was taking advantage of her, after all she was a married woman, and a mother, he stopped. Apologising, he released her from his embrace.

'Please don't apologise,' she whispered, 'it was wonderful.' The whole of her being flushed with desire; no man had ever touched her, held her, kissed her as he did. She had no idea that Gareth had never kissed a woman before. Seeing the longing in her face, he kissed her deeply for a second time.

'I wish for there to be many more such occasions.' His voice, trembling, filled with hope.

Gareth was beginning to feel overwhelmed by what had just happened, feelings that where alien to him. He made his excuses to leave and, climbing into his car, he drove to the top of the road on which the cottage stood, pulling over and stopping the car. Burying his face in his hands, he sobbed, his feelings rolling over him like thunder, the release of emotions – love, passion, and guilt intermingled – reducing him to the wreck of the man whose tear-stained face stared back at him through the mirror. Never before had he experienced such an outpouring; control was his strength, a strength that he learned as a little boy locked in a dark cupboard under the stairs of his parents' grand home, the strength that kept him together.

In the wake of his stepfathers treachery Gareth resolved to branch out on his own, and to that end he entered into talks with a variety of legal people looking to make names for themselves; he was only interested in the best, those hungry for success. Once he had his team primed, he would have a party at his home to introduce them to their colleagues and launch his new venture. During their next lunch together, Gareth invited Lisa to attend his little soiree.

'What will you do about the food?' she inquired, glowing with pride. Attention to detail was her forte where food was concerned.

'I will hire caterers to sort it out,' he answered casually. Convincing him that she could do a better job than any caterers and for half the price, it was agreed that she would be allowed free rein. While he didn't wholeheartedly embrace the idea at first, believing that she worked hard enough, he did see an opportunity to ease her financial situation by paying a decent sum for her efforts. Lisa had worked for Gareth seven and a half months now, and he had never been happier. He was looking forward to the party and introducing her to his colleagues.

Gareth marvelled at the wonderful spread Lisa had prepared, pride of place taken by a large roast turkey and silverside of beef for them to carve as they pleased. She laid out platters filled with a cornucopia of tasty morsels to tempt even the fussiest palate. She arranged and rearranged until everything was perfect to her eye. Gareth had made sure there was a well-stocked bar that would grease the wheels of camaraderie for those in attendance. The scene was set as his guests arrived, ten of the sharpest legal minds around. Steve Ferzackerly and Ray Arrowsmith were the first to arrive. Steve had known Gareth since middle school, both meeting up with Ray at Cambridge University, where they studied law together.

Gareth beamed as he introduced Lisa to them, her charms not going unnoticed by Steve as they hugged her in turn. She wore a black calf-length pencil skirt, black high-heeled court shoes and a cream short sleeved blouse that was tucked in at the waist and opened to reveal a delicate camisole top beneath, showing just the right amount of cleavage. Her thick highlighted locks framed her face and cascaded over her shoulders. Gareth's gaze was never far from Lisa during the course of the evening, watching as she circulated. She was stunning, yet her naivety, which was part of her allure, needed his protection as she was swimming with the sharks. Steve made a beeline for her as she alighted on the large, comfortable plush couch. Sitting closer he draped his arm around her shoulders – he had been drinking solidly all evening freeing his inhibitions. He found her to be an absolute delight and, emboldened by the drink, he flirted with her as Gareth watched from across the room.

Lisa excused herself, heading towards the door that led to the stairs. As she took the first stair she was pulled back and pushed up against the wall. Steve had followed her and was intent on taking a taste of this delectable morsel.

'Hi gorgeous, can I give you a hand?' He pushed his body against Lisa's just as Gareth came round the door.

'Go away,' Lisa laughed, unaware of the implications, thinking Steve harmless, just wasted, as she would put it.

Gareth gripped his arm, making Steve flinch. 'Leave her alone,' he growled.

Steve, holding his hands up, capitulated. 'Ok mate.' Turning, he watched hungrily as Lisa climbed the stairs. Turning back to face Gareth, smiling, he said, 'I am going to bed her before the night is out.'

Steve's feet didn't touch the ground as he was man handled back into the lounge. Gareth called Ray over, instructing him to 'Get him out of here before I do.' Ray knew better than to question an order and loaded Steve into the taxi that he had called. The evening went without further incidents and was declared a resounding success by all in attendance. As the last of the merrymakers left, Gareth and Lisa were faced with the debris that they had left behind. Lisa started to collect the empty plates.

'Leave that, I will sort it out tomorrow. Come and sit down.' Gareth grabbed her, and pushing her down on the couch he started to kiss her. God, how he wanted her, his growing erection bearing witness to that fact, taking his breath away. He consumed her greedily, wanting to possess every inch of her. Standing he reached out and took her hand. Rising to her feet, she followed him, her whole being intoxicated by his touch.

Heading for the stairs, he paused, and turning to Lisa softly said the words, 'You just have to say no.' She smiled and squeezed his hand. Heartened by her response, he led her up the stairs to his bedroom. Gareth had never known this level of intimacy with a woman, his virginity still intact. He was frightened, visibly shaking; he wanted every moment to be perfection, to give her what she desired, to satisfy her every need. He faltered for a moment, hearing his own trembling voice say, 'I have never been with a woman, Lisa, I am a virgin.'

She laughed, replying, 'Right, Lynette was an immaculate conception too.' How could this beautiful Adonis of man still be a virgin, she thought. Smiling weakly at her she immediately knew it to be true; his expression said it all. She pulled him toward her, kissing him hard and full. He responded immediately. God, how she loved this man – he was everything she had dreamt of, yet she always settled for less than she deserved. She took his hand, placing it on her breast. He kneaded her gently, smiling cheekily, but this wasn't enough – he needed to feel the soft skin of her breast against his hand. Pushing his hand inside her top he brushed his fingers over the hard nub of her nipple. She grabbed his shirt at the waist, pulling it free. He instinctively raised his arms over his head, then realised she would not be able to reach up that far; bending forward he pulled the shirt over his head, revealing his ripped torso and muscular arms. Running her hands over his flat washboard stomach she leant forward, taking his nipple in her mouth, licking, sucking, teasing, driving him wild. He threw his head back and moaned. He was barely holding on, his orgasm's aching insistence rising in the pit of his stomach. Carefully he removed the blouse and camisole top, and fumbling with her bra he released her perfect breasts. Unable to take his eyes from them, he caressed ever inch. Lisa worked quickly, undoing the clasp at his waistband and unzipping his pants. Pushing her hand inside his briefs she grabbed and held his steel-hard cock, stroking, kneading, caressing his balls, relishing every moan he uttered. His building orgasm was reaching critical mass.

'I am going to explode, it's too quick,' he gasped. Lisa smiled, her eyes sparkling. 'You're wicked,' he gasped, smiling his sexy come-hither smile. He pushed her onto the bed, removing her skirt and panties, pulling them down over her raised legs, his greedy eyes taking in her every curve. He pulled her naked body upright towards him. Turning her round, he kissed her neck, running his hand down the full length of her body, his erection nestled between the globes of her buttocks. His fingers stroked her denuded mons, penetrating her pouting, warm, juicy cleft, rubbing her clitoris rhythmically. Lisa pulled him onto the bed, spreading her legs. Gareth removed his jeans, taking hold of his engorged cock and pushing it deep into Lisa's hot, soft, inviting depths, the sensation almost sealing the deal. Summoning every ounce of restraint, he pushed himself deeper, wildly kissing and caressing her body as he shook. Lisa, feeling him tremble, pushed him over onto his back and impaled herself again on his rigid cock, riding him deep and hard towards his release. Gareth moaned out loud, his whole being totally overwhelmed as his seed flooded into the safety of Lisa's keeping, his eyes filled with tears.

As they held each other in the afterglow of their love, Lisa leant forward, looking into his eyes. she smiled and said, 'Did the earth move for you?' totally disarming the situation for Gareth, dissolving them both into hysterical laughter. Luxuriating in the feel of each other's bodies, they lay together for some time before Gareth exclaimed that he had never felt anything like that before in his life. Lisa found the revelation hard to accept, but he continued to say that he had heard his colleagues discuss oral sex and had wondered what they were talking about, referring to it as a blowjob. 'So you won't have experienced oral sex at all then?' she quizzed. He shook his head. 'Let me sort that out for you now then.'

The gleam in her eye and look on her face jumpstarted his erection, filling his eyes with wonder. She kissed and sucked her way down his torso, reaching for his hardening cock with one hand, his balls with the other, and gently squeezing them she lowered her mouth, easing his foreskin back, engulfing the end of his cock. Running her tongue over the domed head and rubbing the lip of his glans with the tip of her tongue, squeezing, kneading, sucking, driving him over the edge as he grabbed at the bedding, he came, filling her mouth as he ejaculated.

'Oh my god, I am so sorry,' he gasped, 'I lost it completely,' feeling the colour burning his cheeks he blushed and kept apologising. Not Lisa's favourite part of the evening, but she discreetly deposited his ejaculate at the top of his thigh, reassuring him that it was fine. He reached for a tissue from the bedside drawers, wiping the offending deposit away. He pulled her into his arms and held her close, wrapping himself around her they drifted off into a deep, contented sleep.

As dawn broke, Lisa stirred, feeling hot and sticky, Gareth's body coiled round her like a boa round its prey. In tune to her movement, his eyes opened, filled with lust and longing. Lisa smiled. 'Would it be ok to have a shower before I go to the horses? I am feeling hot.'

'Not nearly hot enough yet. Let's sort that out, shall we?' As he rolled over her with a smile that could charm the gods, she reached down between his legs to discover his rampant member.

'Oh, you're feeling perky? Then let's try something different.' She pushed him away and, turning over, rose to her knees, presenting him with the delectable rump that he had always desired to sink his teeth into. She wiggled it provocatively at him, trying to ease the anxiety she knew he was beginning to feel.

As she looked over her shoulder at him he could see the wicked glint in her eye, which made him think 'Right, lady, game on.' Grabbing her hips he sank his teeth into each perfect globe, making her squeal with delight. He couldn't hold back any longer, sinking his throbbing penis deep into her, far deeper than before. Lisa pushed back against his hard body as he powerfully chased his release. Totally spent, he slumped on the bed, playfully pulling Lisa towards him.

'Come on, shower now, I need to go to the horses.' With a pout befitting a toddler deprived of his favourite plaything Gareth followed Lisa into the wet room. He pushed his body against hers, soaping every inch, his erection hardening yet again, pressing insistently against her rump. 'Steady tiger, behave yourself,' she chuckled, 'I'm leaving.' With that she stepped out from under the flowing water, hearing his hysterical laughter at her corny quip. They dressed quickly together, and as she made to leave, he took her in his arms. Holding her face, he kissed her with a passion that took her breath away. She floated to the stables to feed her horses and turn them out to pasture, breezing through the mucking out, filling their hay nets and preparing the feed for their evening meals. Leaving, she went to her parents' home, where she had been staying due to a trial separation from John. He had stopped her taking Lynette with her, insisting that she remain with him as leverage for Lisa's return. John adored Lynette, his little princess, as did his parents, who indulged her to the point of ruination. To that end he would leave her with them while he went out on the town, making merry. Lisa got wind of the fact that John was passing Lynette around to all his relatives – she wasn't wearing that under any circumstances. She intended to talk to him when she could catch up with him, as he was avoiding her.

Gareth had heard of a farm out at a place called Fence near Burnley that bred sports horses, his desire to hone his riding skills and also to spend more time will Lisa taking precedence. He didn't have the space to keep a horse, his intention being to put the youngster at the livery yard where Lisa worked so that she could back it and school it at her leisure. Lisa had agreed to cast her expert eye over his final choice. The place looked clean and tidy, and the horses were fit and turned out in good order. Gareth's final choice was a leggy black 17.2 hands tall thoroughbred cross Irish draught gelding. He paid the £ 1500 price tag and Jake was loaded into the horse box and transported to the livery yard. As Jake was lead from the horse box, ears pricked, snorting, surveying his new home wide-eyed, Lisa thought him magnificent and spirited. She couldn't wait to get him started but needed to give him time to settle in. Gareth watched Lisa as she walked Jake round the paddock, marvelling at the sight, how totally at ease and in tune she was with the huge animal, Jake following her like a puppy dog. Bursting with pride, Gareth wanted to introduce Lisa and show off his new purchase to the only members of his family that he loved, his Nana and Gramps Baxter. They had been his haven, his refuge from the torment he suffered from the age of four up until the age of 12, when he moved in with them full time. They were totally unaware of the cruel acts that their grandson had suffered at the hands of their daughter and her husband, and it was on the understanding that it remained that way that his mother allowed him to move in with the Baxters.

Gareth beamed as his grandparents' vehicle pulled into the stable yard. Lisa was grooming Jake, making him gleam. They had arrived earlier than arranged, eager to meet the woman that their grandson had talked nonstop about for weeks, the only woman he had ever known – to their knowledge – the reason he was so happy. Lisa stopped grooming, walking across the yard to where Gareth and his grandparents stood. Nana Baxter was an attractive, slender grey-haired lady with a pleasant, heart-warming smile. Gramps was tall and thin with a thick mop of white hair and a stern demeanour, yet his face lit up with a smile as he greeted Gareth. Lisa hugged Nana Baxter who hugged her straight back, beaming all over her face.

'I have heard a lot about you, my dear,' Nana said with a soft voice. Lisa hugged Gramps.

'You have got yourself a grand girl there, my boy,' he said as he turned to Gareth, who flushed coyly.

'Yes, I know.' Lisa returned to the stable and, untying Jake, led him out into the paddock at the centre of the yard where she lunged him on the long rein. Impressed at the sight of the magnificent animal and at Lisa's skills of equitation, they watched, heartened by their grandson's choice of lady, feeling more at ease about his future. They too had wondered if he was gay due to his lack of interest in the opposite sex, always being more interested in his businesses. They wanted to know more about her and invited them both to lunch at the Castle Public House, situated at Bridle Mount. They had many questions for Lisa so, 'honesty being the best policy' as Lisa thought, she recounted every facet of her home life leading up to the separation and how Gareth had helped her. They glowed with pride, their grandson being their only joy. Gareth and Lisa were invited to Sunday Lunch and graciously accepted. Nana and Grandpa made their goodbyes, heading home safe in the knowledge that Gareth's heart was in good hands.

The week flew by for Lisa – she couldn't wait to get to the stables, having to get there earlier than usual as the proprietors were heading off to a show jumping competition, leaving Lisa to manage the yard on her own. She was in her element; she had been mouthing Jake, acclimatizing him to having a rubber bit with keys on in his mouth, getting him ready to accept a metal bit on his bridle. This was essential and not to be rushed in Lisa's eyes, as a riding horse with a hard unresponsive mouth was a danger to its rider. The keys encouraged Jake to play with his bit, making it an enjoyable experience. The next step would be attaching the long reins to the bridle, teaching Jake to respond to the lightest touch in his mouth.

Gareth arrived just as Lisa put Jake back in his stall. She emerged from the stable and bent to pick up a bucket; she hadn't seen his arrival. He smiled his come-hither smile at the sight of Lisa's rump stuck up in the air daring him to smack it; the tight jodhpurs left nothing to the imagination, he just could not resist. He planted a full-bodied blow to her bottom, taking her by surprise and making her scream. She shot forward, turning to face him.

'You ought to know better than to hit me when I have a crop in my hand' she threatened, running towards him, producing the crop she had tucked down the top of her boots. Seeing the determination in her face he bolted towards the barn side, stepping past her yet not escaping her reach and the sting of the crop as it hit home. He squealed, the feeling of the bite of the crop on the top of his thighs serving only to fuel his desire.

He felt his erection spring into life. As she ran in through the doorway he was waiting – he grabbed her, pulling her into his arms, he kissed her long and hard, pushing his tongue into the depths of her mouth, biting and tasting her lips. As he lifted her off the ground, she wrapped her legs tightly around his waist, feeling the outline of his hardness against her sex. He walked towards the bales.

'Don't you dare drop me on those, they are covered in spiders!' She yelped in horror.

'Right, against the wall it is then,' he smiled sexily, placing her feet on the floor in a frenzy. It took them seconds to rip the clothes from their bodies. Picking her up and pushing her up against the wall, he rammed his steel hard erection into her sex, taking her breath away. He held her up with one hand, his other against the wall propping them both up. He powered into her depths, sucking and nipping her nipples, driving them both towards their orgasm. Their release overwhelming them both, they held each other shaking.

Lisa broke the silence. 'We are buck naked, if anyone comes into the yard they will get a real eyeful!' She always managed to make him laugh. They dressed, retrieving their clothes from all over the barn, laughing at their abandonment. She adored him with every fibre of her being. He made her body sing in ecstasy; never before had any man worshipped her body as he did. He was a considerate lover, no roll on and off affair for him – he savoured every moment, every touch, every taste. Her heart was his, yet in the depths of her soul she harboured the doubt that she would never be good enough, that once the first flush of passion cooled for him he would look elsewhere and break her heart. 'How could anyone that looked like him, coming from his background, want me and my baggage?' she wondered. Shaking her head, she drove the notion from her mind, dreading the day coming.

Lisa finished her tasks around the yard, feeding those horses that stayed on site. She asked Gareth to feed Jake and put a net up in his stall for him. Just as they finished, all the horses exercised and fed, Ken Hope, the owner of the yard, and his wife returned from the show. He called Lisa over.

'Get these horses back into their stalls and feed them like a good lass,' he chortled, patting her behind with a lascivious grin. Slapping his hand away, Lisa complied. She disliked the sleazy, ruddy-faced lothario's attentions but needed the cash and a place to keep her horses. Gareth watched, the blood rushing through his veins, pounding in his ears, making the arteries in his neck bulge as his ire reached volcanic proportions. As Lisa disappeared with the last of three horses that had been competing at the show, Gareth approached Hope and asked to have a word with him. Hope never missed a business opportunity involving toffs such as Gareth, always ready to fleece them of the contents of their heavy pockets, given the right set of circumstances.

'How can I help you, Mr Edwards?'

'If you touch her in that inappropriate manner again ...' he growled, holding back the heat his temper was generating.

'You'll do what?' Hope said with an ugly smile, looking him up and down.

Gareth pushed him against the wall, his arm across his throat cutting off his air supply, letting the venom flow. 'I will kill you where you stand.'

Hope might have be many things, but stupid was not one of them – he instantly realised the threat was by no means empty. Releasing Hope who, gasping for air, was unable to speak, Gareth made to leave.

'See you on Tuesday, my sweet,' he beamed as he climbed into his vehicle, 'Jake's looking great, good job.' Closing the door, he drove away, his head in the clouds, knowing that this was the woman he was destined to spend the rest of his life with.

Lisa was working away at Honeysuckle Cottage, busy vacuuming the lounge, humming away with butterflies in her stomach, waiting to fall into Gareth's arms when he arrived. She hadn't heard the door open but caught the faintest movement from the corner of her eye. Beaming all over her face, she turned to see Gareth's stepfather standing in the doorway. Her heart sank.

'He isn't here,' she blurted abruptly.

'I have not come to see my son, it is you that I need to speak with,' he responded in a superior air. Brian Edwards stood six foot tall, lanky in appearance with a grey complexion and the bulbous nose of a hardened whisky drinker. His short dark hair, slicked back, looked almost too dark, giving the impression of being dyed. His mean mouthed demeanour used to strike fear into those working for him.

'What can I do for you? Would you like a brew?' Lisa enquired.

Walking into the room, he replied, 'I have not come to exchange pleasantries my dear, I am here on behalf of my wife and myself to let you know that we do not want your type having any association with our son, and to that end we are prepared to offer you the sum of five thousand pounds to cease any further contact with him. You obviously are in need of the money, hence the cleaning job.'

Lisa felt as if her heart had been ripped from her chest and handed to her in stunned silence she stood looking at the loathsome man that faced her, summoning every last ounce of courage, her voice trembling, she replied 'Should that not be his decision?'

'My son is obviously besotted and does not see you for the gold digger you are.'

Lisa caught her breath. 'I think that I should ring Gareth and ask him what he thinks about your offer,' she almost whispered, trying to regain her composure.

'I do not want my son involved in this matter. I suggest that you give my proposal serious consideration.' He turned to leave.

'I don't want your money. I would like you to leave now.' She was praying that Gareth would walk in and confront this vile man. Some 20 minutes later Gareth breezed in. Rushing into his strong arms, Lisa sobbed.

'Hey, hey, what's wrong babe?' he crooned.

Gathering her senses, she looked up into his stunningly beautiful blue eyes. 'I am just having a rough time with Lynette and my mother.' She choked back the truth, not wanting to upset Gareth.

'You can come to me with anything, Lisa, I'm here for you always.'

'I just needed a hug.' She smiled weakly and he wrapped himself around her, pulling her into the safety of his body. He was troubled by her upset but knew she would unburden herself when she was ready. Lynette was becoming fractious, being passed from pillar to post, and wanted her mummy at home with her daddy. Lisa's mother never missed an opportunity to guilt-trip her about Lynette needing the stability of a family and that she should make up with John for Lynette's sake. She finally caught up with John and they sat and discussed their options. He apologised for his behaviour and promised to mend his ways if she would only give him a second chance. He promised to forego his drinking habit and turn over a new leaf. While Lisa thought his promises a little ambitious, to say the least, her main priority was Lynette, who was suffering from the loss of stability in her life, missing her mum – and school, due to John's tardiness. Lisa told him that she would think about it, but that Lynette needed to go with her at once to get her back into a routine that would restore the little girl's wellbeing. Lisa was torn; her feelings for Gareth were real and ran deep, she no longer had feelings for John, but her daughter needed them together. Her mother's constant harassment regarding the subject and Lisa's dislike of hassle were pushing her towards a decision that she knew would have to be made sooner than later.

Ann Edwards had been none too happy when her husband had returned on Tuesday without the matter of the money-grubbing tart being sorted out. 'I will have to resolve the matter myself,' she muttered under her breath when told that no satisfactory conclusion had been reached. There was much more at stake here and she could not afford for anyone to find what went on behind their closed doors, let alone from a cleaner her son would eventually open up to. Ann Edwards was a statuesque five foot seven inches tall, a stunningly beautiful natural blonde with pale blue eyes and a slender form, a definite man magnet, and she knew it. This classically elegant, morally bankrupt woman had learnt from an early age how to use her god given talents to get everything that she needed, and what she needed was wealth and position. She had expensive tastes and, being all about appearance, it came with a high price tag. She had more than her fair share of handsome suitors that had been weighed, measured, and found wanting when it came to providing her with the lifestyle she regarded as a necessity, in fact, her right. She could always discreetly find a handsome toy to play with, should the whim take her. There was a ten-year age difference between Brian Edwards and Ann, yet she found that she was able to tolerate his unpleasant looks and demeanour to be the trophy wife he required on his arm. Brian kept her and provided all that she desired and more. She was not going to risk losing all that she had because her son decided to unburden himself on some scrubber he was obsessed with. She always dressed to impress, and she intended to undermine her sons cleaner in the cruellest manner. She needed to frighten her off and to that end she would sweeten the deal with a hefty sum to prove that she was indeed a gold digger.

As Ann pulled up outside her son's quaint little home, she thought how much better he could do for himself. There was no evidence of Lisa as she entered Honeysuckle Cottage. 'Hello?' she called out, hoping to attract attention to her arrival.

Lisa was upstairs cleaning the bathroom and, hearing the voice, headed down to greet the person responsible. On seeing Gareth's mother her stomach heaved. Clenching her jaw, she calmly said, 'Gareth is not here at the moment.'

'It's you I need to speak to, you tart, sit down.' As Lisa sat, her blood began to boil. 'If you care anything for my son you would leave him alone. He can do far better for himself than you. You are nothing but a scrubber and a gold digger, you will just drag him down. I have come to up our offer to eight thousand pounds for you to leave and never come back.'

Lisa could hear her blood pumping through her veins and echoing in her ears as she listened to the venom dripping from the snake that faced her. Standing, she spat the words, 'I don't have to listen to this shit, get out before I throw you out!' Taking a step towards her accuser, Lisa felt sickened.

Ann soon realised that this woman was not going to be intimidated or bought. Seeing the look on her face, she turned tail and hurried away to her car. Ann prided herself on being calculating and in control, never thinking for one moment that she would actually fail as her husband had before her, being bested by a cleaning woman of all things. Driving to a secluded spot, she stopped and thought back to how she had reached this place in her life and how she fell for the man who still held her heart after 24 years. David Marsden was an incredibly handsome, strong, confident man with film star looks, a local landowner and farmer. The day he knocked on the door of the grand six-bedroom detached house at the end of the tree-lined drive was a day he would live to regret.

Ann opened the door, looking immaculate even though it was eight in the morning. She was ready to berate the man standing there, as the sign by the door clearly instructed service people to use the back door. She took in the body that faced her in an instant and changed her whole demeanour.

'Good morning, madam, I was wondering if you would be interested in daily deliveries of milk and other dairy products to your door from my local farm?'

Her eyes sparkled at the thought of having this magnificent beast available on a daily basis. 'I would indeed,' she smiled. It was then she resolved to have him in her bed at the first available opportunity.

David delivered produce from his farm to many within the community of Hoghton, where he lived, coming from a long line of farmers/landowners he was well respected by all who knew him, regarding him as one of the most eligible bachelors in polite local society circles. Ann had done her homework and quickly deduced that this could well be the man that filled every criteria, the one that could save her from the sour-faced, ill-mannered oaf she was married to, keeping her in the manner that she regarded as her right. David was enchanted by her attention; he had never been pursued by one so beautiful before. He quickly succumbed to her charms becoming a regular visitor to her bed. She found him a powerful animalistic lover, considerate and generous in his lovemaking, so different to that which she had to endure with her husband. She began to fall in love, a feeling that she found alien and disconcerting. As the months passed, she fell deeper and deeper. She started to feel sickly, her breasts became tender and, horror of horrors, she had gained a little weight. For someone who took so much pride in her appearance that was just not acceptable; she would head to the gym as soon as possible, or so she thought until she spoke to Eileen, a close friend: 'Darling, you are pregnant.' Ann's heart filled with dread as the pregnancy kit confirmed what Eileen had only guessed at. Eileen had informed her that David had sold a large parcel of his land to fund the development of his dairy business. This fact diminished him in her eyes; would he be able to afford her and the child she carried? Ever the realist, she resolved to return to the marital bed, as she needed to if she hoped to have any chance of passing the infant she carried off as her husband's; he was many things, but stupid was not one of them.

Ann shook her head, bringing her back to her present predicament. That little bastard had caused her nothing but heartache and pain from the day she gave birth to him. She was not about to allow him to ruin all that she had worked so hard to earn since he came into this world.

Lisa was sat at the table sobbing into her hands when Gareth arrived home. 'Oh my god, sweetheart, what is the matter?'

She stood and fell into his arms. 'Your mother happened.'

'What?' he spat. Lisa decided to come clean and tell him about the menacing visits his parents had paid her. She watched as the handsome face before her changed, the jaw set and lips tightened, blanching white with icy rage as she recounted everything that they had said to her. The veins in his neck stood proud, his vivid blue eyes darkened. How dare they come to his home unannounced and treat his lady in that manner? For that they would pay.

Gareth sat and had his lunch with Lisa; they always ate to-gether when she was at Honeysuckle Cottage. He made sure that Lisa was composed before telling her he had to go sort a couple of matters out. He kissed each of her eye lids tenderly before leaving, the image of her tear-stained face serving as the cat-alyst that fuelled his rage. Gareth had trained from the age of 15 in the martial arts, kickboxing being his chosen discipline. He had reached fifth dan by the age of 23. Added to that was the control that he had learned from the age of four, when his mother started locking him in the cupboard under the stairs for hours on end, up until the age of 11. In his cupboard there was a bucket that served as his toilet, a chair, a tiny table, and a small portable TV. He spent many hours, days even, in the dark prison under the stairs, his stepfather not wanting to see or hear him. There he bided his time and planned his future. To say he hated them both was an understatement. They were all about appearance: the large expensive home filled with price-less objet d'art, the times he was taken from his prison, dressed in the finest money could buy and paraded for all to see, taken to dance and piano lessons (the done thing in polite circles for children from privileged backgrounds), then taken home and put back in his prison.

Of an evening he was taken up to his bedroom, where he wait-ed in dread for the door handle to turn and his mother to enter his room. He would feign being asleep as his throat tightened, a sick feeling in the pit of his stomach as her hand searched under the covers to touch him in a place and manner that was against the laws of nature. He remembered saying 'Please mummy, don't.'

'This is what mummies do and it is our secret,' she replied. Gareth suffered at the hands of his mother in this way for six years and today they would reap the whirlwind that their com-bined actions had created.

He entered the house to be greeted by his mother and step-father. 'What the hell gives you the right to enter my home and intimidate my lady with the offer of payments to break from our relationship?' His voice was clear, steady, and intimidating.

'She is nothing but a gold-digging slut.' The venom dripped from his stepfather's lips.

Emotions that had been buried deep for years exploded. Gareth hit Brian full in the face, knocking him backward followed quickly by a second pile driving action that shattered his eye socket, busting the eyeball and spilling it out onto his blood-stained cheek, his body writhing in agony. Gareth kept coming, kicking the writhing mass at his feet. His mother sprang into action; grabbing a bronze statue, she made to hit Gareth from behind, but he anticipated every move. Even at the height of his onslaught he was aware of everything around him. Blocking her blow, he grabbed her beautifully coiffured hair and dragged her to the cupboard as she screamed and kicked.

'See how you like it, you evil moronic bitch!' he bellowed as he kicked her backwards into the dark cupboard under the stairs, locking the door behind her. Brian had passed out with the pain that ran through every inch of his body and was not conscious as Gareth took his home apart with his bare hands. Ann could only listen to the mayhem that ensued from her prison. It was later estimated that in excess of 200,000 pounds worth of damage had been done that day.

As Gareth left the property, Ann screamed, 'I am going to call the police, you bastard!'

'Oh please do, I am sure that they would be very interested in the catalogue of abuse you deviants have dished out over the years!'

She fell silent as he left the property. The police were informed that two men had forced their way into the property, attacking them, wrecking their home, and stealing, or so the local papers reported. Gareth never heard another thing about it, nor did they bother Lisa again. She was totally unaware of what had happened that day, only that Gareth had said they would not be back.

Gareth had been invited to attend a well-to-do party at the home of Steve's adoptive parents. Unwisely, his parents were away for the evening, turning their home over to the large group of legal young bloods. Lisa was, to her alarm, the only female presence yet again. Gareth had told Steve that he would not attend without Lisa on his arm, that he was not leaving her at home with her violent husband as things were still strained. Steve agreed wholeheartedly; he needed Gareth's expertise, and Lisa's attendance was an added bonus. Thankfully the property next door was empty – the owners had gone on holiday, yet their son had been left behind due to a family argument. He called into the party for all of 15 minutes, during which he spoke to Gareth and Steve, guardedly handing Steve a set of keys. Gareth told Lisa he would be back shortly, he needed to nip out for a moment. She remembered, shortly after his disappearance, the throaty rumble of a muscle car close by as it roared away into the distance. Gareth returned, beaming all over his face with that come hither smile that made Lisa tingle. With the party in full swing, he grabbed Lisa's hand, and dragging her to the stairs he took them two at a time Lisa giggling as she tried to match his stride. Hitting the top stair, he turned and lifted her off her feet into his arms and kissed her with every ounce of desire that pounded through his rippling muscular body. He carried her through the door of one of the bedrooms, and throwing her onto the extra large bed he tore at her clothing, baring her breasts, sucking and biting her nipples. He was determined to control every facet of their lovemaking this time. He did not waste time removing her panties, merely pushing the delicate white triangle to one side as he forced his throbbing rampant erection hard into her sex, making her gasp out loud.

'Oh god,' she moaned as he forced himself harder and faster into her depths. She could feel her orgasm building and gave herself over to the feeling, only to be rolled over and pulled up onto her hands and knees. 'Dear god,' she gasped as he entered her with renewed force. He dug his fingers into the delectable globes of her buttocks, squeezing and kneading her flesh, before his finger sought out her swollen clitoris as he penetrated deeper, rubbing, caressing, enticing. They were beginning to shake as their orgasms started to erupt when he hoisted her into his arms and pushed her up against the bedroom wall, where he rammed into her with such force that she screamed out in ecstasy as he powered on to their release. Totally spent, they collapsed in a heap on the thick plush carpet as he held her close.

Lisa smiled, facing him. 'Wow, it just gets better,' she whispered breathlessly. He beamed shyly. God, how she loved his smile; it could get him anything his heart desired.

The party ended and as they made to leave, Steve took Gareth to one side and asked 'Will Lisa say anything?'

Gareth's look said it all, yet he replied, 'She won't say a word.' Steve knew better than to question his judgement or his word and merely nodded.

The long weekend break had proven beneficial for the couple whose property was next to Steve's family home, returning relaxed and ready for business as usual, but that was soon to disappear as they discovered that their brand-new Blood Red Porsche had been stolen from its garage. The police were involved, taking the names and addresses of all who attended the party; everyone was called to attend the local station for questioning. When Gareth got the call, he drove to the stable to talk to Lisa. He was right to do so, as it was in Lisa's nature to worry about the least little thing and she was being her usual stresshead about the invitation from the police.

'Do you have any idea what it's about?' he queried.

'I guess it was the car that I heard,' she replied, fixing him with an accusing stare. Gareth nodded and explained that the guy who had handed them the keys had been cut out of his fathers will because they didn't approve of the lady he was seeing, saying that she wasn't good enough for him. That had rankled with Gareth, and he agreed to help him out by removing the love of his father's life: his car. All were questioned and all backed up the story that they were all together for the duration of the party and went straight home afterwards. That was the end of the matter as far as the police were concerned; after all, those in attendance were legal people and beyond reproach. This was a fact that Gareth would use successfully to his advantage in years to come.

Gareth prided himself on his expertise with firearms and decided it would be fun to teach Lisa how to shoot targets, so during one of their many visits to Nana and Gramps' farm he undertook her tuition in the empty adjacent fields. He remembered fondly laughing until his ribs ached as the recoil from the shotgun knocked her backwards clean off her feet and her wonderfully infectious giggle as she looked up at him from the ground. She proved to be an accurate shot, although the recoil often caught her off guard. He invited her to go target shooting late one afternoon with Ray and Steve, taking her to a property they told her was derelict. He offered her the shotgun and told her to aim for the window. She loved being with them, it was always exciting, a break from the mundane slog that was her daily life, her only release being with the horses. She took the gun and leaned into the stock, which she placed against her shoulder. Aiming, she fired, the recoil knocking her backwards yet again, making them all laugh.

She heard the glass shatter and turned to speak to Gareth, only to hear him shout 'Run!' Grabbing her hand, the four set off racing back towards the vehicle they had parked down the road. Out of breath with the laughing and running, they carefully placed the shotguns they all carried in the back of the Range Rover. Climbing in, they all dissolved into hysterical laughter yet again at the look on Lisa's face.

'What have I just done?' she hissed at them. 'You told me it was derelict!'

As they composed themselves Gareth said, smiling his wonderful smile, 'That was a brilliant shot! I am so sorry sweetheart, but I misled you. The house belongs to a Justice of the Peace who convicted an innocent man, a man he knew was innocent, our friend.'

Lisa had no idea why, but his smile and words made everything seem fine. She trusted him implicitly. She somehow knew that he would die before he would let any harm befall her, yet still she thought he would be the one to break her heart. In an attempt to make amends for his subterfuge regarding the shooting out of the window, Gareth took Lisa into town to treat her, feeling the need to lavish her with the best of everything she needed. All her wages were spent on her family and animals, resulting in wearing shabby tops and jeans. Never spending a penny on herself, she went without makeup, perfume, and other essentials. He intended to put that right and to that end they visited shop after shop buying jeans, leggings, jackets, T-shirts, trainers, boots, lingerie, perfume, makeup ... Laden with bags, his arm around her waist, guiding her through the crowds, they joined the down escalator making their way to the ground floor of the shopping centre. He always stood in front of Lisa to cushion her fall should she trip. A rowdy group of three youths in their late teens pushed their way onto the escalator behind them, jostling and pushing other shoppers, forcing their way down the steps, too impatient to wait for it to arrive under its own momentum. The first of the youths knocked Lisa's shoulder hard as he forced his way past, causing her to cry out. With lightning reactions Gareth stuck out his foot, tripping the youth and causing him to fall full length down the moving escalator. Stepping over the prone form of the youth as he struggled to get to his feet, a second well-placed kick knocked him flat, winding him. Gareth's action had not gone unnoticed by the two youths who had hung back, not wanting a similar fate to befall them. However, having helped their injured mate from the floor and sat him on a chair outside the ground floor café, they tracked Gareth and Lisa from the shopping centre in order to retaliate. Biding their time, they caught up with the couple, slotting in behind them on the busy main street as other shoppers passed in both directions. Gareth had seen their reflection in the shop windows as they prepared to make their move. The largest of the youths made to hit Gareth with a cosh that he had produced from inside his jacket pocket. He moved forward to deliver his blow, only for Gareth, who had partially turned, to hit him on the side of the head with such force his head hit the shop window. The reinforced glass merely flexed, bouncing the youth's head back toward Gareth, who kicked his legs out from under him, his body crumbling to the floor just as the security guards from the shopping centre arrived. Some of the shoppers behind them had also been travelling down the escalator and had witnessed firsthand the youth's behaviour, clapping at Gareth's lightning-fast reflexes. The guards questioned Gareth as to the reason for his actions, and while he did not feel the need to answer, he did not need the hassle of the police being called. Reaching into his inside jacket pocket he produced his legal identification card, which worked as if by magic. He was told that they would detain the youths and call the police, taking the names of those who had witnessed the whole incident and who were willing to give statements to the police, exonerating Gareth completely. Lisa was mortified, hating any attention that put her centre stage. She was astonished that Gareth took it all in his stride, not at all ruffled by the proceedings.

Jake was proving to be the spirited lad that Lisa had hoped for. He was responsive to the long rein instruction, but she intended to take a full six months to break him using kinder methods than those usually employed for quicker results. She hated seeing animals put under stress and was adamant that she would never use cruelty as an aid in making an animal compliant. She tapped into the animal's natural behaviour using the methods employed by Monty Roberts, the man known as the 'horse whisperer'. Her success rate was unbroken; people with horses that had been backed using less savoury methods were brought to her for their problems to be solved again, bringing much needed revenue into Ken Hope's livery yard. She was working Jake on the long reins when Hope approached her, calling her over to where he stood. Reining Jake in, she walked him across the paddock. She could see Hope scowling as she approached.

'I will not be spoken to in that manner by your toffee-nosed boyfriend,' he blurted out.

'I have no idea what you are talking about,' she retorted, the puzzlement and shock on her face backing that fact up.

'Tell him to back off or he is off,' he barked back at her.

Not taking any more, she promptly replied, 'Tell him yourself,' and turning Jake round she walked him back to his stall, fed him, and settled him with a full hay net. She completed her tasks, knowing full well that Hope had no grounds for complaint. Her care of the animals staying at his facilities was faultless, her reputation with the horsey set renowned, having had many famous show jumpers given into her care when competing at local shows.

Gareth was acutely aware of the pull little Lynette had on her mum and that Lisa was torn. Lynette wanted her mummy at home with her daddy and was having tantrums when left in her grandmother's safekeeping, needless to mention that Lisa's mother always laboured the fact that she should do right by Lynette and reconcile properly with John, that the child needed them to be together and that she was suffering. Lisa started to take Lynette to Honeysuckle Cottage while she was cleaning, where she met Gareth, and while she seemed at ease with him she constantly asked to go home to daddy. Lynette had been overindulged by both sets of grandparents, and being daddy's little princess she got whatever she wanted, within reason. Gareth knew what he wanted, and he needed to be open with Lisa. Summoning all his courage, he resolved to go home at lunch time and pop the question. As he drove towards the cottage he rehearsed over and over what he wanted to say, butterflies in his stomach. The confident legal eagle felt like a 17-year-old schoolboy in the first flush of love, the truth of the matter being he *was* in the first flush of love. He had never felt anything like this, yet he knew in his heart that it was right. She had to be his for the rest of his life. He gathered his composure as he entered the cottage, seeing her happy, smiling face. As she rushed to his arms he lifted her from the floor, kissing her deeply with every ounce of passion he felt, taking her breath away.

'Wow, more of the same please,' she beamed, looking up into the handsome face that smiled down at her.

'I have something I need to ask you, sweetheart,' he whispered.

'Oh heck, what have I done?' she quipped, her smart-mouthed witty comebacks always making him smile.

'No, I am trying to be serious here,' he reprimanded, trying to suppress his laughter. She could see that he was indeed serious and was dreading what he had to say; she knew this day would come. 'Will you marry me, Lisa, be my wife and let me take care of you and Lynette?' His relief was evident as he finished his question.

'Wait, wait, what did you say?' She was stunned; this was not what she expected at all.

'You don't have to give me your answer straight away. I am asking you to divorce Metcalf and marry me. I love you so much and want to spend the rest of my life with you.'

Her mind was in turmoil. How could this Adonis want her? After all, even his parents didn't think she was worthy of him. Who in their right mind would want her and all her baggage? She would be seen as a gold digger, she had nothing, came from nothing. Lynette would never accept him as her daddy, she cried constantly for John and wanted them back together for good. Her voice trembling, she said, 'Please don't ask that of me, Gareth, I love you, I do, but I have a little girl to think about,' her insecurities flooding her mind.

His heart sank, yet he wasn't giving up without a fight. He had frightened her, that was obvious. He would give her the time she needed, he had caught her unawares. 'Just think about it baby, please,' he pleaded. Taking her in his arms, he held her close, feeling her shake. They held each other tightly, not wanting to let go and face each other, both in their own way frightened of the reality of the moment, minds whirling with uncertainty.

Why did he have to ask, he has spoilt it all, it can never be the same now. The thought played over and over in her head. He cannot mean it, he doesn't know what he is asking, he is just proving a point to his parents. They sat and ate lunch, avoiding the issue which lingered like the elephant in the room. She broke the silence. 'You really need to come to the stables, Jake is ready for you to start working with him.'

Gareth was grateful for the change of subject and smiled. 'That is great news, what is the next step?' The relief in his voice evident, her eyes sparkled, hiding the pain she felt deep inside.

'We need to get you on his back. I have done most of the donkey work, all in all he has been a good lad, hasn't lost any of his spirit though so you need to be on your top game. He will test you, that's for sure.' She smiled at the thought.

He kissed her deeply and held her as he was leaving to go back to the office. 'I do love you, my darling,' he whispered in her ear.

She looked up into his vivid blue eyes filled with hope and longing. 'Right back at ya handsome,' she grinned, defusing the moment instinctively. 'Will Friday, Saturday and Sunday at the stables to sort you and Jake out be ok?'

'It's a date babe, will see you there,' he answered as he left the property.

Lisa sat at the table. Burying her head in her hands she sobbed, heartbroken. She loved this man with a passion she had never felt for anyone before him, and yet her little girl's heart was being torn in two due to her mummy and daddy not being together. She felt nothing for John, who had made no effort to mend his ways that she could see, yet she owed her little girl the best beginning in life a mother could give. It was that resolve that made her mind up to return to John and finish working to devote time to Lynette.

Gareth drove back to work. His heart ached; he had made a total mess of the whole thing with his clumsy approach. He could have kicked himself. He needed to give her time, he knew his love for her would win through eventually. However, little did he know just how long that would take.

Friday was a lovely sunny day, ideal for being out with the horses. Jake was on his toes, prancing and snorting, full of the joys and gleaming in the sun as Lisa led him from his stall into the main paddock on a head collar and lead rope. Gareth was bringing the bridle and saddle that he had specially made for Jake, bringing the saddler to the yard to take his measurements. He wanted everything to be right, only the best for his boy. Lisa took pride in the way she brought young horses on, always using kind methods. Not one of her charges had been head shy or suffered with hard mouths. Today would be a test of Gareth's skills as a rider. He arrived beaming all over his face, always happy to be near Lisa and especially now that he was able to spend three days with her doing what she adored. It filled him with admiration and love.

Tying Jake up, she ran to greet Gareth, jumping into his arms and nearly knocking him over. Wrapping her legs round his waist, she could feel his growing admiration, to which she quipped, 'I can feel you are pleased to see me.' He threw his head back and laughed, she always lifted his spirits and made him blush. He smiled his come-hither smile, the one that filled her with desire. 'Forget about that until later, tiger, we have work to do.'

Lisa fitted the lunging cavesson and rein for better control. Handing them over to Gareth, she instructed him to use his voice to give the commands that he would initially use, such as 'whoa' and 'walk on.' Gareth lunged Jake round the paddock, getting him used to the sound of his instructions, and Jake did not disappoint, being responsive to his voice. Lisa then showed Gareth how to tack Jake up so has not to spook him and to go easy when tightening the girths. This was something that Gareth would know, already being a rider, but extra care needed taking or all Lisa's good work would be out the window. Lisa replaced the cavesson and line so that she had control of Jake if needed, getting Gareth to lay over the saddle in order to get Jake acclimatised to the change in weight, as she had been the only one on his back so far. Jake shot forward, throwing his head up and snorting at the weight of this new being on his back. Gareth hung on until Jake settled, becoming accustomed to the pressure on his back after a couple of circuits of the paddock. Lisa halted Jake and told Gareth to throw his leg over carefully and lean forward, as he was also much taller than she was, and she could see Jake looking over his shoulder at him. Sitting up carefully, Gareth slipped his feet into the stirrups, mindful not to use any leg aids until Lisa gave him the go ahead. Jake started to prance and snort, full-spirited and raring to go. Gareth had an excellent seat on horseback, sitting deep in the saddle, Lisa thought, walking Jake round the paddock until he stopped prancing and walked on in a collected manner. Removing the cavesson line, she handed over total control to Gareth.

'Take it gentle on his mouth, he is very sensitive so no hard pressure.' Lisa instructed.

Gareth applied the slightest pressure with his leg and Jake shot forward at a pace. He reined him back again using the minimum of pressure, and he was so impressed at the way the young horse responded to him. What a fabulous job Lisa had made of the magnificent youngster! Lisa watched as Gareth put Jake through his paces, glowing with pride at the progress they had made. Jake was sweated up with the stress of the new stimuli he had faced, so Lisa called time.

'That's enough for today, he is still just a big baby. We can do more tomorrow.'

Gareth nodded. Dismounting Jake, he removed the saddle and walked him round the paddock to cool him off before returning him to his stall to rug him up and feed him. He turned to Lisa and said, 'I have prepared a lovely evening for us as a thank you for all your hard work, sweetheart.'

She smiled her coy smile with that wicked glint in her eye. Oh my, was he going to take care of that for her later. He returned the favour with a smile that took Lisa's breath away with expectation. The journey from the stables to Honeysuckle Cottage that day was a blur, Lisa following Gareth at speed in her Alpha Sud. As she followed him into the cottage, she marvelled at the beautifully arranged table set before her, cut blooms arranged to perfection as a centrepiece, surrounded by scented candles.

'I thought we might eat first,' she heard him say from behind her.

Giggling, she dived at him, wrapping her legs round his waist. 'No, I don't think so.'

The wicked glint in her eyes signalled 'game on' as they tore at each other's clothing, both having been in a heightened state of arousal at the stable. High on what they had achieved with Jake, Gareth high on the thought of possessing the beautiful talented woman who had stolen his heart, Lisa needing to feel his touch and take her fill of him before she said her final good-byes. The meal was forgotten in a haze of passion; they didn't make it to the bedroom but rolled naked onto the couch, clothes in tatters on the carpet, kissing, caressing, biting, kneading, sucking, lost in a frenzy of carnality. He pulled her onto the coffee table, pushing her legs apart and throwing them over his shoulders. He started at her breasts, driving her wild with the sensation of his tongue on her nipples, working his way down her body, nipping and licking. Reaching her sex, he pushed his fingers deep inside, searching for her g spot while he licked and sucked at her clitoris. His rhythmic persistence driving her over the edge, he felt the pulse of her release on his fingers. In a flash she pushed him down onto the coffee table, reversing the roles. He perched at the end with Lisa knelt between his legs, stroking his perineum, squeezing his testicles, applying gentle pressure. Revelling in his gasps and moans, she eased his foreskin back, working her tongue hard against his frenulum. Building the friction, she eased the foreskin back and forth.

'Oh, dear God,' he gasped as he ejaculated, Lisa squeezing his testicles, intensifying the force of his semen hitting the back of her throat. Gareth had never felt such intensity in his release; he wanted more. He grabbed her and kissed her hard, tasting his come on her lips and tongue. He scooped her up, cradling her in his arms, the warmth of her naked body pressed against his own as he carried her up the stairs to his bedroom.

He threw her on the bed and opening the top drawer of the bedside unit produced a vibrator. His cheeky grin said it all. 'How do you want this?'

Her eyes sparkled at his ingenuity. How had he plucked up enough courage to go and buy it? she mused, giggling at the thought. She opened her legs. 'Use your imagination,' she purred.

Gareth's eyes lit up with lust as he switched the rigid phallus on, its gentle hum resonating, rubbing its tip over and over the lips of her sex, watching the ecstasy on her face as she closed her eyes, giving herself over to the sensation. He moved it over the swollen nub of her clitoris, her hips raising to met the probe again and again. Her panting and moaning telling him she was close to the edge, he pushed it deep into her juicy cleft, switching the setting up. The hum became more insistent. He licked and sucked at her clitoris.

'Oh God,' she moaned. Hearing Lisa invoking the deity, he removed the vibrator and pushed his now rock hard, aching member deep inside her, driving with an urgency that built to a frenzy. He pulled her up into a kneeling position, and grabbing her long thick locks, pulling her head back, he rammed deeper, still holding her in place with his hand tangled in her hair. He powered on and on until they both succumbed. Totally spent, they collapsed into each other's arms. On this occasion, she had no witty comeback, no smart-mouthed quip; she just wanted to be lost in his arms, loved, safe, totally fulfilled. They slept tight in each other's arms, lost in their love.

They had a busy day in store and an appointment with Jake to keep. 'Come on, you,' Lisa beamed, 'we need to get going, shower time.'

He rolled over, stretching. Watching her glorious nakedness walk towards the wet room, his eyes filled with lust. In a shot he was behind her. Assuming his favourite position behind her, his manhood standing proud nestled between the globes of her bottom, he soaped her breasts. Working down the full length of her body, he eased his fingers into her sex, gently pressing her clitoris as he bent and kissed her neck, nipping her shoulder. She responded with a long deep moan, and turning she jumped up to wrap her legs around his waist. He made to catch her as she slipped slowly down his body, the soapy foam making them both way too slippery. They fumbled, slipping about on the wet room floor, landing in a heap; he had made sure that she was safely on top of him. As they dissolved in hysterics, he pulled her to her feet. Making a feeble attempt to dry each other, his erection was getting in the way.

'I think he wants something,' Lisa smiled, nodding in the direction of his manhood.

Grinning from ear to ear, he threw her over his shoulder and carried her to the bedroom, spanking her bare bottom for good measure. He threw her on the bed and was about to dive on top of her when she parried.

'Don't take all day, we have a horse to train,' she giggled, scrambling up the bed, only to have her ankles grabbed. Being pulled down the bed toward him, she tried to kick out but his grip was way too tight. Her struggle only served to heighten his resolve. He grabbed her thighs, forcing her legs open.

'You are going nowhere, lady,' he growled as he forced his steel hard member into her cleft, powering hard and fast into her, causing her to cry out in ecstasy. He paid no heed, biting, sucking, nipping, forcing himself deeper and deeper until they both exploded.

He wrapped himself around her like a python, holding her tight until they recovered their composure enjoying the afterglow of their passion. 'How about we jog to the stable?' he suggested.

'Good idea, let's go.' She was up and dressed in no time.

They ran side by side, matching each other's stride, covering the two miles to the stables in no time at all. Jake was waiting, fresh and raring to go. Gareth tacked him up, taking care not to startle the youngster, while Lisa tacked up Teddy, a 16.2 hands retired hunter that was steady. It was his job to give Jake confidence, as they were taking them out on the road. It was a steady walk, with Teddy on the outside. Jake was on his toes to start with, but soon settled to the job at hand. They laughed, relaxed in one another's company, totally at ease. What could be better than this? Gareth thought. His love and admiration for Lisa knew no bounds. The hour flew by, and returning to the stables they settled their mounts back into their stalls after mucking them out and feeding them. Two star-crossed lovers acting like teenagers, laughing, giggling, enjoying each other. Lisa never wanted this to end, yet knew that it soon would. She had no choice, or so she thought.

Gareth always prided himself on keeping his body in top condition, his martial arts training required the ultimate commitment. He enjoyed pushing himself to be the best at whatever he did, and Lisa's companionship made the whole process more enjoyable. No fool he, never taking on anything that he knew he could not master and be the very best at, his disciplines being Jujutsu, kickboxing, Taekwondo, Karate, and Kung Fu. His particular forte was kickboxing. All required control, the one thing that held him together. Control in all things except one: Lisa. She was his Achilles heel, his only weakness. They worked out together at the local gym, ran, and cycled together. He loved teaching her how to use the handguns; target practice was always fun. They were a perfect match, and yet she knew that it would soon come to an end. She had told Metcalf that until he showed signs of making changes to his lifestyle, she would not allow him to move back home, keeping Lynette at home with her. Yes, he had got another job and was bringing in regular wages – although spraying cars did not pay as much as his former job, it was a start. However, the drinking had not stopped, and it was that which turned him into a violent monster. He had promised her that he would make every effort, but that Rome was not built in a day. She hoped that he would give her an excuse to walk away for good, but Lynette would be the one to suffer and the little girl did not deserve that sort of heartache. She had done nothing wrong but love her mummy and daddy, who no longer loved each other.

Things at the stable had become a little strained. Hope was king of all he surveyed with the exception of Lisa, and especially when Gareth was around, although little was said, Hope being mindful of Gareth's threat and his fast-growing reputation as a tour de force, not backing down from any challenge. This snippet of information had come to Hope's attention during a fact-finding exercise into Gareth's background after their altercation in the stable yard. Hope never said a word to Lisa, being well aware of what an asset she was to the yard; he didn't pay her a penny, just allowed her to stable her horses there as payment, and his yard had never looked better. Lisa took pride in her work; the horses were always beautifully turned out, their stalls immaculate, their tack sparkling, and she exercised his current show jumping team. Often preparing meals for their return from long journeys to events and putting the horses away, bedding them down and tending to any injuries they may have, bruised legs being the most common, she was someone he could rely on and not afford to lose.

Sunday morning was filled with glorious sunshine, and the sound of laughter carried on the gentle breeze as they tacked up their mounts to do more road work. Jake was being unusually stroppy, prancing, snorting, and foaming at the bit. Gareth couldn't understand what was wrong.

'It's your electric arse,' Lisa grinned. 'Get off, let me show you.' Gareth dismounted, giving Lisa a leg up onto the magnificent animal's back. Immediately his whole demeanour changed; he was quiet as a lamb, standing patiently. 'There. told you.' Gareth frowned. 'You have a deep seat, which is excellent, but you have only ridden hacks that have had hard mouths and needed constant digs to keep them moving. This guy is fresh, sensitive to your every touch and movement of your backside on his back. Keep your leg aids lighter,' she instructed.

Swinging her leg over, she slid from Jake's back to be grabbed and kissed on the forehead by Gareth, who gave her a leg up onto Teddy, who had been stood patiently waiting, steady as a rock. In two easy graceful moves Gareth was back in the saddle, Jake snorting with indignation. Arching his neck, he strode forward, following Teddy's lead. They walked to a bridleway that led to an open gallop.

'Let's see what this guy is made of!' Gareth called from behind her. She could hear Jake snorting and as she peered over her shoulder, she could see him prancing sideways behind her. Even Teddy had realised it was time for fun. She was just about to say it was way too soon when Jake shot past her, bucking, Gareth grinning all over his face as the mass of untapped energy he sat on dropped into top gear and took off.

'Come off and I will kill you!' she screamed after him, her words lost in the rush of air. Teddy was not having that young whipper snapper making him look shabby; he only needed to be asked once and it was all there, his speed was breath-taking. Lisa loved this old lad, he always gave 100 percent, gaining ground on the youngster and almost pulling level.

Jake could see Teddy coming up on his flank, and quickly taking it up a notch he accelerated away. 'Yes,' Gareth growled as he felt the power of Jake's acceleration beneath him. After ten minutes of flat-out racing Gareth pulled Jake up, acutely aware that he must not push the youngster too hard, Lisa quickly joining them on Teddy, both animals full of the joys at being allowed to open up and let go.

'You have done a great job with him, sweetheart,' Gareth gushed, catching his breath. She blushed at the compliment, confident in her ability. Horses were her passion and she had the best animals to work with.

'Let's get back,' she smiled, 'they need to cool down.'

As they entered the yard Jenny Hope, Ken's wife was stood hands on hips, looking annoyed to say the least. 'I would like a word with you, Lisa,' she barked. 'Come and see me when you have put your horses away.' Gareth shot her a withering glance, at which she smiled sweetly, having a thing for that particular young man – he could do no wrong. Little did she know that he hated the sight of that type of woman, the same ilk as his mother: all for show.

Lisa left Gareth to sort Jake out and walked across to the stable office where Jenny sat waiting to pounce. 'What the hell do you think you are doing feeding other people's horses for them? It is part of the service we offer, and you are doing me out of money when doing it for them as a favour.'

'They leave it out for me, all I do is put it in the stall, I can't see the problem – they buy their hay and straw from you anyway?' Lisa questioned her logic, thinking it odd that she should only bring the matter up now when she had always done it.

Jenny had been picking at things Lisa did of late; she was very jealous, being aware of the attention Ken was paying Lisa. 'Don't let me catch you doing it again,' she snapped at Lisa. The threat was empty, as Jenny knew that she would catch it in the neck from Ken if she dismissed Lisa for a minor infringement.

Lisa returned to Jake's stall to help Gareth finish bedding him down. 'What did she want?' he enquired. Lisa explained what had just happened. Gareth's reaction was one of anger and dismay. 'Would you like me to have a word with her?' he asked, trying to hide his distaste at the thought of being face to face with the woman in a confined space. The mixture of her perfume with a certain body odour turned his stomach, reminding him of not being able to escape his mother's malodorous scent during her visits to his bedroom. That particular odour triggered the same violent response, making him physically vomit throughout his adult life, especially when women came on to him. Lisa assured him that she could handle anything that Jenny dished out, so he took a step back, relieved and satisfied that his lady love was quite capable. 'How long has that been going on?' he enquired.

Lisa laughed, recounting a trip to a show with a full team that required her assistance, an A level show jumping competition with many world class riders being present. Ken had been driving the horse box and called out to Lisa to come sit next to him, only to be hijacked by Jenny, who exclaimed that it was her place to sit there next to him and not a stable girl's. Jenny was jealous of the attention that Lisa received from the riders at the show, who sought her out to see if she would exercise their mounts for them or to help their staff with any problems they were having. Lisa was trusted with thousands of pounds worth of horse flesh from all over the world at many such prestigious events. She bought many customers to the yard, all looking to tap into her expertise, the skills that filled Ken Hope's pockets.

They finished up and had a leisurely jog back to Honeysuckle Cottage. Gareth was primed and ready as they entered the cottage. He had learned that Lisa would not eat before sex, always preferring an empty stomach, so he had prepared everything for their meal and left it in the fridge. They were hardly through the door when he grabbed her. She anticipated his move, jumping into his arms and wrapping her legs tight around his waist, knowing that they were heading for the wet room – showering was part of Gareth's seduction.

'Let's go wash the stables away,' he said, smiling that smile that unlocked everything that barred his way. She giggled like a schoolgirl. They ripped at each other's clothes, lost in the moment. The water washing away their day, he stood behind her – his favourite position – his rock-hard erection firmly in place between the globes of her bottom as he soaped each breast lovingly, working his way down towards her sex, caressing her lips and kissing her neck and shoulders. They stepped from the shower drying each other slowly, rubbing each other's bodies.

He could not contain himself any longer; she was in perfect unison, jumping into his arms and wrapping her legs round his waist. He pushed hard into her juicy cleft, holding her with one arm, the other against the wall, protecting her from banging her head. She clung to his body as he powered into her, taking her breath away. Listening to her moan, he pushed harder, deeper, faster, until he could hold back no longer; he felt her release and exploded.

He had prepared a feast fit for a queen, their candle lit meal the perfect romantic setting. His attention to detail matched that of Lisa. They spent the evening laughing, recounting their day, chatting about Jakes training and Gareth needing to learn how to make the majestic animal change legs, as he aspired to the lofty heights of dressage. Lisa doubted herself; how could she leave this behind? Only truly happy when with him, longing for him when not together, he was her deepest love, yet she knew in the darkest recesses of her soul she would never be good enough and he would find this out and break her heart. She could perhaps stay with him a little longer ... she needed his love, his sex, no other man made her body respond with rapture or ache with longing for his touch as he did.

They spent the night wrapped in each other's arms, delighting in each other's touch, intertwined, worshipping each other's bodies, lost in their passion. The following morning, they woke, untangling their bodies. They made their way to the wet room, their lust for each other still in a heightened state – they could not get enough of each other. Gareth had never had the rush of sexual fulfilment before Lisa; the thought of self-gratification filled him with disgust, making his stomach retch – he associated it with the disgusting acts his mother carried out, and he steered clear of any woman that came onto him, as that elicited the same reaction. For the first time in his life he was freed from the grip of disgust and self-loathing that had marred his life from childhood. Lisa was the one that healed that pain and made it right.

Lisa had never experienced the intensity, the adoration, and the freedom that she felt in Gareth's arms or the power that he put into pleasing her. She was his focus, it was all about pleasing her; how could she walk away from the one man that truly loved her, body, soul, heart, and mind? They luxuriated in the feel of the water cascading over their nakedness. Lisa threw her head back against his chest as he soaped her breasts from behind, working his way slowly down her torso, fingers searching out her swollen clitoris, caressing it lightly, increasing the intensity of his touch until she moaned.

'I want you,' he whispered in her ear.

Nuzzling his neck, she could feel his hardness against her thigh. Turning to face him, Lisa jumped into his arms, wrapping her leg around his waist. The force of her jump knocked him off balance, and they fell to the wet room floor. She impaled herself on his erection, hearing him groan at the force of her pushing him into her depths. She pulled her feet under her, and knees bent she rose, easing to the end of his throbbing erection. She began a rising trot, pushing him deep, forcefully, violently, making him cry out in ecstasy and pain as she picked up speed, driving them both without mercy toward their orgasm.

'Oh dear God,' he gasped, 'where the hell did that come from?' She looked exhausted, having giving it every ounce of her being. Her legs ached, turning to jelly as she tried to stand. 'You nearly snapped my dick off,' he said, grinning, his eyes wide with wonder.

'I just needed to let go,' she replied coyly.

'You need to let go more often then,' he smiled – that smile, the one that could melt the hardest heart and open every lock that barred his way, yet it would only ever be for her, his one and only, his soul mate. They looked into each other's eyes adoringly, the water cleansing their passion. They kissed fully, deeply, tasting each other as they lay on the wet room floor, relaxed, thoroughly spent.

'We can't stay here all day.' Lisa broke the silence. Gareth jumped to his feet with cat like ease and pulling her upright they continued their shower like two teenagers, laughing, wrestling, and splashing each other.

Dried, dressed, and ready for the day, Lisa looked in the mirror. 'Just look at my hair! I look like Crystal Tipps from the cartoon,' she gasped. She scraped the masses of thick curly locks back and up into a ponytail, using one of the many scrunchies that seemed to breed in her pockets.

'You look amazing, babe,' Gareth cooed.

'Yeah right, you lie so well.' Her smart-mouthed retort made him laugh out loud. They parted with a kiss that always took her breath away.

Lisa headed off to her home to meet up with John, who was dropping Lynette off. She had moved back into her own property with Lynette, while John remained at his parents' home. Her theory had worked: since she had returned home with Lynette, the little girl's schoolwork had steadily improved and there were fewer tantrums, although she did miss her daddy being there. The ball was squarely in John's court, he needed to stop drinking before she would allow him home – she would not submit her little girl to the sort of violence that she knew he was capable of. Lynette hugged Lisa so hard that it made her feel guilty for her time away. She felt as if she was caught in a tug of war that would shatter her heart into a million shards. Lisa had heard of a property that was coming up for sale on the road where her parents lived – if she could sell her property, she would only need a small mortgage to secure the purchase, which would make life a lot easier, her mother being nearer. That also suited her mother, as Lisa's baby brother needed minding on occasion; they worked on a quid pro quo basis. She had spoken to John about it and with his blessing she set the wheels in motion. Her property sold within the space of a week, being offered the asking price without any reservations. Lisa was elated. Her new home was a large family semidetached that needed some work, but she loved the challenge, and it would be left entirely up to her make the place her dream home.

The following morning was Honeysuckle Cottage day. It lifted her heart; she felt like a teenager with butterflies in her stomach at the thought of seeing him again, the anticipation almost proving too much. Gareth intended to have extended lunches from now on – he planned to have far more than just lunch when Lisa was at his home cleaning. He was a late starter where sex was concerned, due to his childhood trauma, but had read every manual on how to please his lady love, although unable to look at the illustration and pictures contained in it. Pornographic images from videos were also off the menu as a learning aid, as the images made him violently ill, yet he could not get enough of Lisa. She dominated his every waking thought, he physically ached with longing for her. He took pride in being the master of anything he undertook, and she deserved the very best he could be.

There were tell-tale signs even then of what was to come, yet Lisa was so caught up in the rapture of their love, never having known such intense passion and from such a stunning gladiator of a man. Her naivety made no allowances for what was hiding in the darkest recesses of Gareth's psyche, the titan that would eventually straddle and dominate both legal and criminal worlds, Lisa being the catalyst that set his journey in motion.

He breezed in through the door, bringing with him the energy and excitement he was feeling. His lunch was waiting, a beautiful salad, the table set with flowers. As Lisa turned to face him, he scooped her up. She instinctively wrapped her legs around his waist, immediately feeling his steel hard erection, and giggled, clinging to his body as he mounted the stairs two at a time. Throwing her on the bed, he tore at her clothing, baring her breasts. Pulling her jeans and panties down, he bit her inner thigh hard, making her cry out. She slapped him hard, serving only to drive him into a frenzy. Biting her breast and unzipping his pants, he released his erection. Throwing her legs over his shoulders, he pulled her towards him, impaling her, thrusting hard and fast. She gasped, her eyes wide, trying to catch her breath. He paid no attention, totally lost in his mounting release. Powering on and on, he felt the spasm of her release, giving him the signal to erupt with such force he cried out.

Her smart mouth could not resist the opportunity. 'Oh my god, who had his Irn Bru this morning, then?' As he lifted his head to look at her, she could clearly see the outline of her handprint on his cheek. 'Oh no, I am so sorry, I have marked your face,' she apologised.

'Don't apologise babe, it was a turn on. In fact, I would like more of it.' Grinning from ear to ear, he grabbed her legs, pulling her down the bed to reinitiate their connection.

'Hang on a minute, your salad is going cold,' she laughed, kicking out at him. She grabbed her jeans and ran for the stairs.

Beating her to the landing, he grabbed her and kissed her, tasting her lips, nibbling and sucking, making her feel that she was the only woman in the world. Handing her the panties she had left behind, he patted her bare bottom as he walked past her, heading for his lunch. Lisa went to the bathroom to wash and dress, joining him for the lunch she had lovingly prepared. They revelled in each other's company, always laughing, chatting about all manner of topics. They complimented each other perfectly; she was the glove made to fit his hand. Gone were all thoughts of leaving him behind, living for the moment; the future was not yet a reality. He floated back to work, lost in a haze of fulfilment, glowing in the realisation that she would be his.

Lisa had decided that she needed protection in her new home for herself and Lynette, not trusting that John could maintain his promise. To that end she decided to purchase a puppy of a breed that would eventually keep them both safe: a Dobermann puppy. Tarron, a big, bold, black and rust male puppy of eight weeks old, who breezed in and took over. Lynette adored him as much as her mother, and the little girl's confidence and demeanour came on in leaps and bounds with his arrival, as he became her focus. Both Lynette and Tarron visited Gareth's home occasionally as Lisa went about her chores, Gareth becoming enraptured with them both. Lisa's work with Jake had been a resounding success and in a few short months Gareth had become totally bonded with the magnificent steed. She found Gareth to be an attentive and accomplished pupil, taking her instruction forward and becoming adept at dressage to the point of being ready for competition. Nothing looked more magnificent than Jake, with Gareth onboard, working through their dressage routine. Lisa watched Gareth in his tight jodhpurs that left nothing to the imagination and well-fitted black competition jacket that accentuated his broad sloping shoulders and formidable arms. He was never short of female admirers at the yard as he put Jake through his paces, yet was oblivious to their presence, only aware of his lady love as she watched proudly. Jake proved to be a very level-headed ride, his only vice – if you could call it a vice – being that he hated to be passed by another horse, which suited Gareth down to the ground. He revelled in Jake's turn of speed, giving him the rush that he craved in all things.

As the weeks passed, Gareth's lovemaking became more adventurous, wanting to please Lisa in every way possible. His lunch breaks become two hours in duration, not one, but then he was the boss, and no one would dare pull him on that issue, or any other for that matter. Even at university they always followed his lead and never challenged his judgement; he was the boss then and remained the boss for the duration of his life. He quickly became known as a top criminal defence solicitor, the one man you needed to get you out of your predicament, earning him the nickname of 'Mr Fix It.' He never lost a case for that would be a failure and that just would not do at all. Having been told continually that he was a failure by his mother and stepfather his mission in life was to prove them wrong. His stepfather had withdrawn his tuition fees during his first year at university, leaving Gareth without lodgings and food. It was only due to the fact that he was always top of his class that the University saw fit to offer him a full scholarship, recognising his potential. Steve and Ray stuck with him through thick and thin, marvelling at his resourcefulness, their loyalty to him making the bond of their friendship unbreakable. His connections on both sides of the law became legend, respected and feared in both circles as the man not to cross, the man that succeeded where others failed.

Steve and Ray were never far behind him, all three graduating with top honours from Cambridge. All three had suffered horrendous sexual and physical abuse as children and been failed by the system, a system they came to know inside and out, a system that they intended to make pay for its shortcomings. They mirrored Gareth's expertise in martial arts, all three training at the Dragon Club in Cheshire, reaching the top grades possible in the United Kingdom at that time. To go further they would have to be invited to train at the Shaolin temple in the region of Song Shan Mountain in Dengfeng City, Henan province; only those at the top of their game were considered. Gareth represented the club in competitions and rose to the top, being undefeated in the country. During a competition bout with a team from Russia Gareth's opponent lost control, throwing the rules out of the window, dangerously attacking. This forced Gareth to defend himself using a kick that snapped the man's neck, an injury that he never recovered from, rendering him paraplegic. That incident served to end Gareth's competitive career; he was not prepared to put himself in a position that could end someone's life for the sake of having the competitive edge. That, however, would not be the case should he have to defend himself or his loved ones in their daily life. His reputation, with the passing of time, was that of one who showed no mercy if challenged or attacked.

Lisa would often accompany Gareth jogging round the country lanes near his home. He used exercise to keep his body in peak condition and to prevent his demons from escaping. She enjoyed being at his side, there was no place that she would rather be, so she made the most of the time she had left with him. They jogged five miles in the warm summer heat and stopped by a bench to re-hydrate. Lisa's shorts were extremely short, showing off her glorious rump, which had not gone unnoticed by the man jogging behind them.

As he drew near, he stopped, bending to tie his laces. He ran his hand up Lisa's bare legs, stroking her bottom. He laughed. 'These just draw you up.'

In a microsecond he was lying unconscious on the ground, the words having barely left his lips before Gareth connected with one punch, so fast that Lisa didn't see it hit.

'What the hell, is he ok?' The alarm in her voice was obvious.

Striding over the prone figure, Gareth replied coolly, 'He will be fine, come on, let's get back to our jog.'

She looked at him, astonished. 'Why did you do that?' she asked, not sure what it was that he had done.

'No one touches my lady in that way, he was out of order and his actions totally inappropriate.' Gareth's voice was cool, calm, and unruffled. He started to jog back towards his home. Lisa, at peace with the justification he had given, followed in his wake.

Lynette was at Lisa's mother's after school, where Lisa headed to collect her, being met by her mother's look of disapproval. Lynette had been in trouble at school, having a hissy fit which warranted a letter being handed to her grandmother when she collected her. 'You need to get this child home and John back where he belongs, she is beginning to suffer emotionally. You think more of the damn horses than you do of your daughter,' she barked. 'Sort yourself out, my girl, or I won't look after her again.'

Lisa knew she could not hold John off any longer: he had not taken a drink in a while, a fact that his family bore testimony to. Her mother hammered home the guilt trip, forcing Lisa to make the move she had been dreading. Lisa had told Gareth of Lynette's growing emotional problems and that she needed to be there more often. He had not realised where that was leading.

Lisa had spoken to John, and it was agreed that he would move back into their home within the next couple of days. As she entered Honeysuckle Cottage for what she knew would be the last time, her heart was breaking, waiting for Gareth to come home for lunch. He breezed in, high on life, to find Lisa stood with her back to the sink, eyes red from the many tears that she had shed on the way to the cottage. His heart sank.

'Babe, what's the matter?' He covered the space between them in a nanosecond, wrapping his arms around her.

She struggled to free herself, knowing that she would be unable to do what she must if he held her close. 'Please don't, Gareth, sit down, I need to talk to you,' she gasped, her words catching in her throat. He knew then that his world was about to be torn down around him. His shoulders slumped, he sat heavily in the chair. 'I am going to go back to John for no other reason than Lynette needs to be with us both as a family. I cannot go back to him and continue to work here with you, I will only want more, and that cannot happen if I am to make it work for Lynette.' She looked across at him, the tears streaming silently down his face.

'Please, Lisa, don't do this, I beg you, don't leave me,' he sobbed, his head now buried in his hands, his heart shattered into a million tiny fragments. She rose and wrapped herself round his shoulders her head next to his he turned in his seat, arms around her waist, head buried in her chest. They cried together, neither wanting to let go. 'I understand your reasons for doing this, just give me one day a week, that's all I ask,' he barely caught his breath, 'let me make love to you one last time, please Lisa.'

'I can't go back and make a go of it with John and come here to you, I would not want to go home. I have to make a clean break Gareth.' She saw a broken man through her tears, lost in the debris of his dreams. 'You will find someone else to love you in time, you are gorgeous, and I will always be there for you if you want to talk.'

'I don't want anyone else but you, there can only ever be you in my life, you are my world, don't take that from me, please.'

Lisa kissed him deeply, passionately, as if this was her last day on earth. The bittersweet taste of their tears lingering on her lips, she grabbed her coat and placed the keys to the property in front of Gareth on the table and walked out of Honeysuckle Cottage and Gareth's life for the final time.

Gareth's colleagues had not seen him at the office for two days and his staff had questioned his absence, which set alarm bells ringing. Steve and Ray climbed into the firm's Range Rover and headed for Honeysuckle Cottage. The door to the property was unlocked. All the curtains were drawn, the rooms in darkness. Pulling back the curtains to shed light on the proceedings, they headed for the lounge, which smelt like a brewery, Gareth's body prone on the couch, face down, arm dangling on the floor, and by his hand laid his Colt 45 handgun. On the coffee table, empty and laying on its side, was a bottle of 11-year-old Lagavulin the Managers Dram malt whisky that had cost him 595 pounds, a second empty bottle on the floor under the table.

'Christ almighty, man,' Steve exclaimed at the sight and smell. Ray stood in shocked silence. This was not the Gareth he knew, he never lost control like this. He was out cold. Their attempts to rouse him failing, they grabbed his legs and torso and heaved his dead weight up the stairs to the wet room. Propping him up against the wall on the floor under the shower head, they turned on the cold water and stood well back. They could not comprehend what had happened to reduce him to this; he rarely drank for the sake of control alone. He would allow himself the occasional glass of the finest malt whisky, paying as much as 2700 pounds per bottle to savour the silky-smooth sting at the back of his throat as it warmed him. 'Why put a thief in your mouth to steal your words,' he would say as he watched those around him getting drunk and spouting rubbish.

'It must have been pretty bad, whatever it was.' Steve offered his take on the matter to Ray, who nodded in agreement. They heard Gareth spluttering as the cold water shocked him back to consciousness.

He sat for all of ten minutes under the numbing cold of the water as he remembered where he was and – 'How the hell did I get up here into the shower?' he spluttered. His eyes starting to focus, he could see the outline of two men. 'Steve, Ray, is that you?' Coughing, the water choking him.

'Yes, we are here,' came the reply.

He stood unsteadily, using the wall to balance, his clothes soaked to his skin. 'You could have taken the suit pants off lads, that's a bloody good Armani suit ruined,' he complained.

'A 'thank you' would do,' Steve replied, smiling.

'Make me a strong black coffee please,' he instructed Steve, who raised his eyebrow. Coffee was another 'no-no' – things must be bad. Ray followed Steve downstairs to clear away the bombsite that Gareth had left in his wake.

Peeling away the wet clothing, he turned the water to hot, climbing back under the jet. He remembered the feeling of desolation as he put the barrel of the gun in his mouth, ready to end the pain. As he started to put pressure on the trigger, he heard Lisa's voice sob, 'You promised me you would be here for me and you lied.'

'That's right, I did promise you that, my world, my soulmate.' He dropped the gun to the floor and started to drink until he passed out.

Dressed and showered, he appeared downstairs. The lads had cleaned up and his coffee was waiting. They were the only two who would dare and even be allowed to ask what was going on, so he pre-empted their questions. 'Lisa is gone,' was all he said. They knew then it would be folly to question him further; those three words said it all.

'There is a backlog of case work at the office,' Ray informed him, 'what do you want me to do with it?'

Gareth pondered for a while, then replied, 'I will be back in on Monday, there isn't anything that won't keep until then. Have you got your trainers and tracksuits with you?'

They nodded, always having spare clothes for every occasion in their vehicles. Finishing his coffee as they changed, his head pounding, he took four bottles of water from the fridge, drinking one down and handing the others a bottle each. He ran that day like a man possessed, pounding the pavement, pushing every last ounce of effort from his aching body. They kept pace, covering a good 15 miles, stopping only to re-hydrate and ending up back at Honeysuckle Cottage.

Lisa was making every effort to put the pieces of her relationship with John back together – she even accompanied him on one of his drinking forays into town, for what it was worth. She found herself sat talking to a complete stranger who she thought was quiet, chatty and pleasant, while John chatted to his cronies, oblivious to the fact that the stranger that had homed in on Lisa had far from honourable intentions. However, there was one pair of eyes taking in every nuance and movement from across the large, crowded bar who knew exactly what the stranger had in mind.

Lisa, who was a little worse for wear, having partaken of a few beverages to numb her return to John's bed, excused herself to the stranger and weaved her way through the crowd, out of the bar and into a corridor that led to the restroom. She had only taken a few steps towards the ladies' when the stranger who had tracked her from the bar grabbed her arm forcibly and slammed her against the wall, pushing his hand up her skirt and down the front of her panties. Pinioned against the wall by his weight, she could not move, her struggle against him was futile.

Before the stranger was able to achieve his goal the door to the corridor burst open. In seconds Gareth had the stranger by the back of his neck, spinning him around, his arm pressed across his throat, the man fighting for air. Gareth beamed at Lisa. 'Are you ok sweetheart?' She nodded, in shock at his appearance. 'Do what you have to do, I will deal with this.'

When she returned, Gareth was waiting. There was no sign of her assailant. He hugged her close and asked if she was ok, and she nodded sheepishly. 'I could see what he was after. You need to take care, there are a lot of predators about.' It seemed like it was a blink of an eye, and he was gone, just as dramatically as he had arrived; it was all a little hazy in Lisa's mind.

Lisa was finding it difficult to continue working at Hope's livery yard as Ken's advances had become a problem in the wake of her split with Gareth. Jenny was becoming obsessed with the idea that they were having an affair. Lisa had three young horses at the yard at that time and she would need to find another yard that would be prepared to offer her the same terms. It didn't take her long; her reputation opened many doors where horses were concerned. Ken Hope took great pleasure in informing Gareth that Lisa was no longer taking care of Jake and that he had appointed a replacement for her, revelling in their break-up. He got more than he bargained for.

'Do not let anyone near that horse. I will be down to collect him in two hours.' Gareth ordered, to Ken Hope's utter shock. True to his word, the horse box arrived and Gareth loaded Jake, taking him to Nana and Gramps farm. Hope's business began to suffer as the news of Lisa's departure filtered down through the horsey set's lines of communication, many following Lisa to the new yard at Black Brooke Farm.

John had accompanied Lisa to Hope's yard to help her load and move her horses, and Ken could not miss what he saw as an opportunity to cause problems for Lisa. He engaged John in conversation, telling him how pleased he was that Lisa had seen sense, breaking up from her toffee-nosed boyfriend and returning to him. John had been blissfully unaware of Lisa's relationship until that moment; the very thought of it sickened him. He would keep that snippet of information filed away until he needed it.

Lisa had been back with John for four months when to her dismay she fell pregnant. She found that sex with John was more of a chore and that she needed to be anaesthetised with drink to get through the ordeal, thankful that it only took a matter of minutes before he rolled off and fell asleep. She longed for what she had left behind, thinking of Gareth constantly; at times tears would come flooding from her wounded heart and overwhelm her. She must stay strong for Lynette and keep her word to John to try and make it work. He had started to drink the odd can at home but had so far kept his word and stayed clear of his old haunts. Lisa was dreading telling John that night, but she didn't expect the reaction that she got.

He had eaten the tea that Lisa had dutifully prepared, and Lynette was staying the night at her grandparents'. He was sat in front of the TV, a four pack of lager on the floor by his chair. Lisa sat on the couch. 'I have something to tell you, John,' she said quietly.

He finished his first can and started a second before he turned to face her. 'What is it?' he enquired, trying to look interested but just wanting to wash away the stress of his day with alcohol.

'I am pregnant.'

The words shocked John into giving his full undivided attention. 'For fuck's sake, that's all we need!' He was almost shouting, the anger in his voice clear and present. 'Get rid of it, we can't afford another.' His words gutted Lisa. All life was sacred to her and she had no intention of ripping the child she was carrying from her womb for him or anyone. 'Don't think you are keeping it, you get rid of it as soon as possible.' He was adamant. He kept looking at Lisa with total disgust throughout the evening. Finishing his cans, he headed out the door and she knew then where he was going.

He didn't come home that evening at all. Lynette was his little princess, his only love, and he just did not want to love another as he did her. The thought had crossed his mind that the child may not be his but that of the toffee-nosed individual that Hope mentioned to him in passing. As the pregnancy developed, John dismissed that notion from his mind – the timing was wrong – yet he still kept insisting that the child be aborted before it was too late. He had taken to drinking heavily again and stepping out. Gossip filtered down to Lisa that he was sleeping around with some less than savoury individuals, but that he had a predilection for young teenage girls.

After one of his trips to his favourite haunt, he returned home to find the house in darkness and Lisa fast asleep in bed. She was laying on her side with her back to him. He collected a pair of scissors from the kitchen and, climbing into bed, he cut off the back of her waist-length hair, leaving the beautiful tresses laying on her pillow.

'That will teach you, bitch.' His slurred words fell on deaf ears.

The following morning Lisa woke bright and early, shaking her head. Something felt different. She always scooped her hair up into a scrunchie to clean her face and neck. Running to the bathroom, she could see that her hair had been cut. She gasped, 'What the fuck?' Running back into the bedroom, she could see the hair on her pillow. 'You totally evil bastard!' she screamed, startling John awake. 'Look what you have done!'

'What? What are you talking about?' She turned to show him the damage that he had done. 'Oh god,' he sobbed, 'I don't even remember doing it, I am so sorry.'

'You and I are finished! I want you gone from here,' she said, tears streaming down her face.

Climbing into her car she drove to the nearest hairdresser's. The woman that owned the shop had known Lisa from her school days. She could see Lisa had been crying, then she saw the hair. 'Oh my good god, who did that to you?' she exclaimed.

Lisa told her what John had done and asked if she could make it look decent. The woman agreed, saying that it would be lovely when she had styled it. As she left the hairdresser's she drove down the main street, catching a glimpse of Gareth standing outside the offices of a local legal firm. Pulling in, she walked back towards him. She hadn't seen him or spoken to him for almost six months. His face lit up as their eyes met, and he caught his breath. He wrapped his arms around her and hugged her close. She sobbed, feeling safe in his strong arms.

'Aw, babe, don't do that,' he soothed, noticing straight away that her hair had been cropped short. 'What happened to your beautiful long locks?' She told him that John had found out she was pregnant and, getting off his face drunk, he had hacked her hair off. Gareth's blood boiled. He wanted to kill the low life for laying a hand on her, not only for cutting her beautiful hair, but for getting her pregnant. He had obviously not learned his lesson; perhaps he needed reminding. Gareth knew that Lisa was ill when taking the birth control pill and so did John.

They walked to the café on the same street, catching up on each other's news for 20 minutes, enjoying being in each other's company as if they had never left. 'I miss you, my love,' Gareth said as she started to return to her car.

'I miss you every day,' she replied, looking back over her shoulder at him, the tears filling her eyes.

John had gone to his local hostelry straight from work and was weaving his way back to his parents' home, not daring to venture near Lisa after her ultimatum. Gareth walked from behind John and pushed him down an empty side road, his baseball cap masking his face.

'You didn't listen, you stupid little shit, did you?' he growled, his grip crushing the little man's windpipe. With one blow he shattered John's eye socket and broke his jaw, kicking his legs out from under him. John collapsed in a heap. Gareth rained blow after blow down on John's body, leaving him a battered bloody heap. He walked away from John's prone body to the phone box and called the emergency services yet again to tell them where to find the body that he had left unconscious and bleeding.

This time when the Royal Infirmary rang to inform Lisa of John's accident she refused to go to his bedside. She no longer wanted anything to do with him; it never crossed her mind that Gareth was behind both of the most severe beatings that John had taken. Lisa informed the police that John was an aggressive drunk and continually caused trouble at the places he frequented. She supplied them with the names of the bars, pubs, and clubs that he haunted on a weekly basis, telling them she had no idea where he had gone that evening, just that she did not want him back. There were no witnesses to what had happened, but then there never were when Gareth was involved. Always carefully covering his tracks, biding his time, patiently waiting for an opportunity to strike.

Lisa was seven months pregnant the next time she saw Gareth on the main street of Bamber Bridge, standing outside the same legal firm. They hugged and chatted, and as she made to walk away, Gareth caught her arm and pulled her close. 'If you need anything, anything at all, please contact me.' He gently stroked her baby bump and kissed her forehead.

'God, I love you,' she whispered close to his ear as he stooped to kiss her cheek.

John was allowed to come and stay on Friday night to see Lynette but knew that drinking was off the cards, as he had turned up on a couple of occasions stinking drunk and had been sent packing. Lisa gave birth to a second baby girl, Louise, in October 1982. John had been allowed to witness the birth on the understanding that he remained sober while around her. He came to the house to help Lisa when she returned home with her new baby and for a month kept up the façade of being a doting father, but gradually slipped back into his drunken ways. John became obsessed with the fact that Louise was not his, as she bore no resemblance to him, causing him to argue with Lisa; yet another excuse to go out and get drunk. John's father offered to solve the problem by paying for a paternity test, which Lisa confidently agreed to. The test results came back proving conclusively that Louise was indeed John's daughter. John had never wanted the pregnancy; he shunned Lisa when pregnant, telling her it was disgusting. No shows of tenderness by stroking the baby bump, yet became the doting daddy when outsiders were around, unable to maintain the deception for longer than an hour or so. Things improved for a short while after the results proved his theory incorrect.

Louise was three months old when John came home after work one Friday absolutely wasted, stinking of drink. Lynette was being spoilt at her grandparents for the weekend, baby Louise had been bathed fed and was fast asleep in her bassinet, the house was immaculate, cleaned top to bottom, the dog had been fed and walked, and John's meal was ready and waiting. He staggered past Lisa into the house without a word, into the kitchen and towards the sink. The pots were the only things that had not been done; he unzipped his pants and started to urinate onto them. Lisa saw red, picking up the heaviest pan she possessed, thwacking him good and hard at the back of the head. He dropped like a stone.

'You fucking dirty bastard!' she screamed. After ten minutes she began to panic; he hadn't moved 'Oh dear God, I have killed him.' Thankfully, he moaned just as she spoke and started to get up from the floor.

'Get your brat and get out of here or I will kill you both!' he shouted, lunging at her. He stumbled, falling flat on the floor again.

Lisa didn't need telling twice – she knew that he would carry out his threat. In a flash, she grabbed baby Louise in her bassinet and left the house. Where would she go, what would she do? She walked to the nearest phone box and dialled Gareth's number instinctively. His impeccable voice answered the phone and she visibly relaxed.

'I need your help, are you alone?' she sobbed.

'Yes, where are you?' he asked. She told him that she was at the phone box on Brindle Road. 'Stay there, I am coming for you now.'

Gareth was there in a blink of an eye. Jumping out of the car, he took baby Louise from Lisa. Laying the bassinet in the back seat and making sure she was secure, he closed the door. Turning to Lisa, he pulled her into his arms. The stress washed over her as she dissolved into tears.

'You should not have to put up with this, sweetheart.' The soft tone of his voice made her relax. 'Come on, let's get you back to the cottage.'

Lisa told him of John's behaviour up to and including today's incident, watching his face change, his lips white with rage. Arriving at the cottage, Gareth lifted the baby from the back seat and carried her bassinet into to the lounge, laying her on the couch.

'Sit, I will make us a drink.' Lisa looked washed out. He brushed a tear from her cheek, tenderly kissing each of her swollen eye lids. He lifted her chin and kissed her softly. 'Let me take care of you and the baby, stay here with me.' Lisa relaxed fully for the first time in months, knowing that she and the baby were safe and cared for. She nodded in agreement.

'I only managed to grab two bottles and a couple of nappies before I ran for it,' she exclaimed.

'What do you need? Give me a list and I will go for them,' he answered, checking his tone at the thought of her having to run away to save her and her daughter from a beating they did not deserve.

'My purse is at home.' She looked crestfallen at the hopelessness of her situation.

Gareth rolled his eyes at her and smiled. 'I will get everything that you need. You need to rest, you have just had a baby, my love.' He was in his element; he had his one true love back under his roof, by his side once more.

Lisa laughed. 'That was three months ago, it's not an illness you know. I will come with you.'

They drank their green tea and planed a shopping trip for the following day. Lisa had to ring John's parents to tell them not to take Lynette home and the reason why they should take her to Lisa's mothers. His father apologised for his son's behaviour, Lisa telling him that this was the final straw, there was no coming back from this. Gareth listened to the conversation, his heart jumping for joy at Lisa's declaration. Lisa got baby Louise ready for bed while Gareth heated the bottle. Washed, changed, and fed, Gareth carried the bassinet up to his bedroom, placing it on the chaise lounge that faced his bed, making sure that it was secure with its precious contents.

They sat and chatted about their lives during their absence from each other until the early hours. Taking Lisa's hand, he said, 'You need to rest, and I mean rest.' He led her upstairs they undressed quietly so as not to disturb the baby. Climbing into bed, he wrapped himself around Lisa. As they drifted off to sleep, she could feel his need pressing rigidly against her bare bottom. She had not realised how exhausted she had become or how much her home life had taken from her until that moment as she relaxed into a safe sound sleep.

The following morning, Lisa woke to find the baby gone. Jumping up, she hurriedly dressed, running down the stairs. She could hear Gareth cooing and giggling at the baby he had cleaned, changed, and fed a bottle. Lisa marvelled at the sight that faced her, Gareth wearing tracksuit bottoms, barefoot, walking backward and forward, cradling baby Louise in his arms as if it was the most natural thing in the world for him.

'That really suits you, babe,' she smiled, as he blushed at being caught out using baby speak to Louise.

'Go get showered, sweetheart, we have shopping to do for my new friend here.' Gareth beamed with pride has he placed the baby back in the bassinet.

They drove to the main Mother Care store in Preston City Centre. He was like a child at Christmas, much to Lisa's dismay; he bought everything that a baby girl and her mummy would ever need. The Rolls Royce of push chairs for the little princess, a beautiful, ornate cot for the bedroom, along with several beautiful baby dresses for every occasion, leggings and comfortable tops for Lisa, and slippers, sandals, hairbrushes and toiletries. He spent a small fortune, certainly boosting Mother Care's takings that day. Only the best for his girls, he quipped when Lisa remarked at his extravagance.

Unpacking all the goodies was a logistic nightmare, but baby was still asleep, so they got to work. Lisa came across a feeding bra and held it up. 'What, may I ask, is this?' she enquired, grinning from ear to ear. 'It may have escaped your notice, but I am not breastfeeding.'

'Oh yes, I thought it may come in handy when I need a feed,' he blushed, rushing off to assemble the cot for his new baby girl.

When all was unpacked, Lisa realised that she had better products for Louise here than at home. Lisa showed Gareth how to change nappies, prepare the baby's formula and how to bathe her. He took to it like a duck to water, no awkwardness or clumsiness to him. This was natural, how real daddies looked after their baby girls, and he had taken her to his heart just as he had her mother. It never crossed his mind that this was another man's child. She was Lisa's child, and that was enough. Gareth seemed to take it up a notch when caring for his two girls; he took time off from work, allocating his case files to other members of his staff and occasionally working from home, although his concentration never strayed far from Lisa and Louise.

Lisa remembered that she had left Tarron at home with John and that he would not be looked after, so Gareth agreed to take her home to pick the puppy up and bring him to the cottage. The night of the shopping trip Gareth saw to all the baby's needs, putting her to bed in her fairytale cot. He had prepared a candle lit meal for them both and would not hear of Lisa helping in anyway, she had just had a baby, he kept reminding her, as if she needed reminding – her swollen breasts had thankfully started to subside and so had her baby bump, yet she felt a little self-conscious and wanted to move it quickly. They ate their meal, chatting about the best way for her to get back into shape, although Gareth cautioned her about taking it easy at first; after all, she had just had a baby.

'If you say that once more, I will slap you,' she quipped with that wicked glint in her eyes.

Gareth felt his erection stir in his jogging bottoms, which left little to the imagination. 'I know one way to help you get back in shape,' he replied, his face lit up with his world class smile.

'Oh, do you now?'

He pushed her top up and pulled down her bra, uncovering her swollen nipples, which had darkened in colour to a rich red hue. 'They are gorgeous.' His hungry eyes feasted on the sight before him. Putting his face between her breasts, his hands at either side, he kissed and sucked each in turn, making her giggle like a schoolgirl. They had longed for this moment for so long.

Gareth didn't want to disturb the baby in his room, the idea of her watching what they would be doing fazed him. Taking her hand, he led her to the guest bedroom. Opening the door, the scent of cut flowers filled the air, along with scented candles that lit the room. Lisa was in awe at the beautifully prepared scene that faced her. On the bedside unit was a vibrator, a tube of lubricant, and a condom; he had left nothing to chance.

'Oh, definitely premeditated then,' her smart-mouthed retort making him grin.

He scooped her up into his arms and carried her to the wet room, standing behind her, soaping her body, luxuriating in the touch and feel of her skin against his own. This was now an essential part of his seduction. Drying her, he carried her into the bedroom and threw her onto the bed. In a second his naked body towered over her, his eyes feasting on the body that he had yearned for, stroking her curves.

'You are gorgeous,' he growled seductively. He pushed her legs open, dipping his tongue into her sex, sucking her clitoris.

She moaned as he stroked and kissed her baby belly. 'Don't, it's ugly,' she whispered.

'There is not one thing about you that is ugly, my love, you are beautiful.' He always knew the right things to say to boost her confidence, a far cry from the treatment meted out by John. Collecting the vibrator from the bedside unit, he turned it on to the highest setting, running the tip around her clitoris and up and down her labia, his fingers searching out her g-spot, pressing and rubbing it deep within. She was lost in the torrent of sensations and emotions that ran through her body. How she had longed to feel like this again; only with him did her body respond in this way. She needed to feel him deep inside her, connected, complete, and he did not disappoint.

Gareth had pent up all his feelings, having had no release since she left his employment, unable to indulge in self-gratification, a legacy from the abuse he had suffered at the hands of his depraved mother. He could hold back no longer. He rammed his steel hard erection deep into her with so much force she cried out. He powered on relentlessly, holding back his orgasm with every fibre of his being. They rolled off the bed onto the floor, where she mounted him, impaling herself on his rigidity, riding him until her legs turned to jelly, their orgasm flowing through their bodies, building in intensity. As they started to tremble in unison, he scooped her up into the kneeling position. He pushed deeper, harder, faster than ever before, his hand tangled in her hair. Feeling the rush and pulse of her orgasm, she reached between her legs, grabbing and squeezing his balls as he exploded into her depths. She heard him cry out as he flooded her with his seed, the force of which was in danger of bursting through the condom that had been hastily applied.

They were totally spent, no witty remarks forthcoming. Lisa felt completely safe in the only arms that she ever wanted. 'I love you, babe, with every fibre of my being,' he whispered, kissing her forehead.

'You are my love and always will be, no matter what happens.' She almost sobbed the words. They lay together, always with her back to him, his erection nestled constantly between her buttocks, one arm wrapped over holding her breast and the other under her head. Holding each other like this, they drifted off into a deep sleep.

Gareth had set the alarm for three am, the time baby Louise was programmed to wake for a feed; the bottle already prepared, he had covered all the bases. As Lisa made to climb out of bed, he halted her. 'Get back into bed, I have this under control,' he smiled, 'you need to rest–'

'Finish that sentence and you're dead,' she laughed.

'I said I've got this, now get into bed,' he ordered.

This set the standard for the rest of the time she spent at Honeysuckle Cottage: she was not allowed to do anything, Gareth totally took over the baby's care, making Lisa rest as much as possible. She felt useless. That was her job, not a man's job, the years of conditioning from her mother playing in her head, mixed with guilt and the nagging doubt that he was too good for her. Even his heartfelt words could not ease the doubts she felt.

Lisa's mother was furious at having Lynette dropped off at her home. In her mind Lisa should put up with John's behaviour at all costs for the sake of their children and be at home where she belonged. As Lisa hung up the phone, her ears still ringing with the sound of her mother's incessant harassment, she turned to find Gareth facing her, cradling baby Louise in his arms. What a perfect picture that made. Was it so wrong to want happiness and fulfilment for herself? she wondered.

'I will have to go and pick Lynette up within the next couple of days. She isn't happy about my being here with you.'

Gareth nodded, rocking back and forth cooing at the baby. 'When you're ready, take my car and go for her, I will look after Louise.'

During the course of the next few weeks Lisa was not allowed to do a thing. The house was immaculate, Gareth saw to that; he prepared all their meals and took extra special care of the baby. Lisa's time was taken up by Gareth's needs. He wanted to possess her body constantly, and when not buried deep inside her he had to be close to her, touching, stroking her, kissing her neck, kneading her rump, running his hands up and down her thigh ... she had never had that sort of attention in her life before. She luxuriated in his touch, yet by the end of the three weeks she was beginning to feel as if she would suffocate. He did everything for her, every time she turned round he was there, making her feel trapped. Her only release from his overpowering presence was when she went to the stables to feed and muck the horses out. He would take Louise while she went to sort the horses out, even then turning up with the baby, Tarron walking to heel, to watch her work. He always turned up, no matter where she was or what she was doing. Lisa never gave it much thought before, as she was so in love; she did not see the warning signs until years later. She had gone from a relationship with someone who didn't give a damn to one who worshipped her. She wrote what she was feeling at the time off as her having to make adjustments between the two extremes.

Borrowing Gareth's car, she drove to her mother's to collect Lynette, with every intention of taking her back to Honeysuckle Cottage. Lisa's mother was waiting to pounce when she arrived, unleashing a tirade of abuse aimed at eliciting pangs of guilt. She grabbed Lynette and her clothes, taking her back to the cottage. The little girl was upset at her grandmother's outburst but soon settled down when Gareth bribed her with a brand new dolly called Barbie. Barbie had many accessories that accompanied her, keeping Lynette busy. He smiled, knowing that his attention to detail had won the day, although this proved to be short-lived as come bedtime Lynette cried for her daddy nonstop, waking the baby up. Lisa promised Lynette that they would go home the following day and that she would see her daddy then. That seemed to work and eventually, exhausted, they all fell into a deep sleep.

Lisa didn't hear the three am alarm, waking at seven to find Lynette and Louise bathed, dressed, fed, and playing happily in the lounge. Louise was giggling away happily at the mobile of unicorns and rainbows that hung above her head in her push chair. Lynette was dressing her Barbie doll in one of the many outfits that she had.

Looking up, she shouted, 'Mummy, can we go home and see daddy now please?' running towards her mum, arms outstretched. Lisa nodded, looking at Gareth's face; his expression said it all. Lifting Lynette up, she noticed that the little girl's cheeks were flushed.

Feeling her head, she remarked, 'This little girl is burning up.'

'We will take her to the doctor's then.' Gareth replied.

Loading them into the car, they drove to Lisa's doctor's surgery, where it was confirmed that Lynette had a high temperature due to an inner ear infection and that she should be kept from school until it came back down to normal. They collected the prescribed antibiotics from the chemist, and on the return journey Lisa told Gareth that she needed to collect the children's things and get home, dashing his hopes of her moving in with him. He nodded his acceptance of the situation, even though his heart was breaking, his mind in turmoil.

As they loaded the last of their things into the car, Lisa broke down, falling into Gareth's arms. They sobbed. 'Please, Lisa, don't leave me,' he pleaded. She could not reply choking back her tears. Their hearts broke for the second time as Gareth dropped them at their home. He kissed her goodbye and drove away.

Lisa's relationship with John was on a knife's edge, yet she allowed him to return to the house as Lynette was poorly and wanted her daddy. She made him up a bed in the spare room and he was under no illusions that he was there for the children and only the children. His drinking habits had not disappeared, he had merely become more adept at hiding it. He was trusted with minding the children, but only if Lisa was certain he had not been anywhere near drink. On one such occasion, Lisa was called to a problem with one of her horses with suspected colic, trusting John with the task of bathing Louise. Unknown to Lisa, John had smuggled drinks into the house and hidden them, and as soon as she left he started to consume them. When bath time came around, he was intoxicated. Running the bath, he omitted the cold water. He undressed baby Louise and lowered her into the hot bath, failing to test the waters temperature. The poor little mite screamed in pain as he immersed her lower body in the hot liquid. As Lisa came through the door, all she could hear were her baby girl's screams. She took the stairs two at a time, bursting through the bathroom door. Knocking John over, she grabbed the baby, immediately running her lower half under the cold water. Luckily, this stopped the skin from blistering.

'You useless fucking drunken idiot!' She screamed at the top of her voice. 'Get out of my house and don't come back!' Staggering to his feet, realising the enormity of what had just happened, he left Lisa to deal with the aftermath of his actions. She filed for divorce at the first available opportunity, giving John supervised access to the girls of a weekend. Lynette was now old enough to have an opinion and chose to stay with her paternal grandparents on the weekends.

Lisa had only limited contact with Gareth as the months passed, the whole emotional rollercoaster proving too painful. They limited themselves to the occasional phone call, which always ended in Gareth telling her that he loved her and missed her. It had been six, maybe seven months since the last call when the phone rang.

Lisa, lifting the handset and hearing the deep, clear, cultured tones, caught her breath 'Hello babe, just wanted to know how you are and if you need anything.' Gareth's voice had taken her by surprise.

'Hello, sweetheart. It's been a long time, I have much to tell you.' She told him of the divorce and how John was not paying maintenance, resulting in her taking on yet more jobs. As the conversation came to a close, he told her how he missed her and loved her. 'You need to find yourself a lovely lady without all my baggage, Gareth.' She spoke almost in a whisper, the words physically hurting her heart.

'Please don't do this babe. I will wait forever if I have to,' he sobbed.

'I will be here for you if you need me, Gareth.' She choked back the tears as she hung up the phone.

Gareth's life was on auto pilot; he had cut back his emotions, not wanting to feel anything, making him hard to be around. He had many female admirers that made advances towards him, much to their regret. He was none too polite in his dealings with them, his brutal words cutting them to the bone. He only wanted one woman and he would wait for as long as it took or go to his grave without her. The girls in his office knew exactly how to deal with him, keeping out of his way unless he required them to carry out tasks, which they knew had to be done quickly and efficiently. He was in his office when the phone rang.

'I have your grandfather on line one, Mr Edwards.' the telephonist imparted.

'Hello Gramps, what's wrong?' he questioned.

'It's your Nana, my boy, she has had a stroke and it's not looking good.' The old man choked on the words.

'I am on my way Gramps, with you in 20 minutes.'

Nana Baxter never recovered from the stroke she suffered, dying peacefully in her sleep, leaving Gramps a lost, devastated, broken man. Gareth had lost the only women that loved him and hugged him up until Lisa came into his life, the only woman he trusted until Lisa. He felt a dark emptiness inside that was ready to consume him. He put on a brave face, trying to help Gramps to adjust, but the old man had given up; his soulmate gone, he had no wish to endure without her. Gareth needed the one person that he knew he should not contact, yet she was the only one that could ease his pain. He knew where Lisa would be, having followed her covertly on her daily routines for some time. He drove to the yard where she kept her horses, having moved them there after the trouble at Hope's yard. She was shocked to see him, his face drawn, eyes swollen from crying.

'I am sorry to do this, but I need you, can I speak with you?' he almost begged.

'Oh my god, what has happened?' she exclaimed, rushing towards him, arms outstretched.

'Nana has died, Lisa,' he sobbed into her neck as she hugged him close.

'Oh babe, I am so sorry,' she said, her eyes filling with tears at the news and the hurt Gareth felt.

'Can we go somewhere please?' he asked, not wanting anyone to walk by and see his distress. She nodded her assent, climbing into his car, and drove a little way down the road. 'I can't face the funeral on my own,' he said, the words catching in his throat.

Without hesitation, she asked, 'Can I be there for you?'

He knew she would never let him down. He longed for her touch, just hearing her voice eased his pain. His visit was brief; he was in danger of losing control and that must not happen. He asked her to meet him at Gramps' home, kissed her tenderly on the forehead, and dropped her back at the yard. Driving away from her was the hardest thing for him.

The day of the funeral, Lisa made her way to Gramps' place, where Gareth greeted her. Pulling her into his arms, his heart shattered with the loss of his Nana. Lisa was devastated at the sight of this powerful titan of a man reduced to tears, her heart ached for him. She loved Nana deeply; the wonderful lady had always treated her with kindness, welcoming her into the family as a daughter-in-law. Composing themselves, they went to join Gramps, who hugged Lisa and dissolved into tears, unable to cope with Lisa's show of tenderness. Lisa made a welcomed brew to steady the nerves for the ordeal to come.

They had hardly finished their drink when the funeral cortège arrived. Both men choked back their sobs as they walked out to take Nana on her final journey. Hoghton Parish Church was packed with those wishing to pay their respects to a lady who was well thought of and loved within the community.

Gramps had prepared a eulogy for his lost love, and had managed to hold it together until he started to read his words out loud. Breaking down, he sobbed, 'I loved you so much, my darling. I can't do this.'

Gareth rose to his feet, painfully aware of his grandfather's struggle. 'It's ok Gramps, I will read for you,' he said, his voice almost a whisper. Lisa walked forward, wrapping her arms around the old man's, leading him back to his seat.

Gareth struggled through the rest of the eulogy, tears streaming down his face, making it difficult to see the written word, yet having committed it to memory he managed to finish word perfect. So many people offering their condolences, mourning the passing of a great lady and a lovely human being. One notable absence from the poignant proceedings was the woman who called Nana mother, too ashamed to attend because Nana had discovered some of the harm that she had inflicted on Gareth as a child, although not all of the horrors.

The wake was a grand affair, all in attendance catered for in style. It was a long yet comforting day, filled with many wonderful stories of Nana's life and of those whose lives she had touched. As the mourners slowly filtered away, Lisa started to clear away the tables where the funeral feast had laid, only to be stopped by Gareth. Gramps had gone to rest his head, the day having taken its toll both emotionally and physically.

'Leave that, I would like you to come to the cottage with me, just for a chat,' he pleaded. His entreaty tugged at her heart strings; his heart leapt as she agreed.

She followed him to the place where it all began. How she had missed the scent of the honeysuckle that greeted her. Gareth prepared her a drink and they sat together going over the events of the day. He could hold back no longer; his strength failing him, he let all his pent-up emotion flow, a melding of loss for Nana and for Lisa. He fell into her arms and she held him closely, tightly, as he sobbed, breaking his heart for his only love to see. She held him for what seemed like an age, knowing instinctively that he needed to heal his pain.

As he tried to compose himself, Lisa rose. Taking his hand, she almost whispered in reverence, 'Come with me.' He followed her up the stairs into his bedroom. This was like no other time, they undressed each other carefully, lovingly; this was making love to heal all wounds. They worshipped each other's bodies, tenderly caressing each other. The intensity of their connection overwhelmed them both as they lay in each other's arms, listening to the rise and fall of their breathing as the stress of the day lifted from them and disappeared.

'I can't let you go, babe.' His voice wavered.

'I have to go, my love, I have a babysitter with the girls and I have to get back.'

They dressed in silence, hardly able to bear their goodbyes. As she walked through the door of Honeysuckle Cottage, there seemed to be a finality about the moment that made him catch his breath as he watched her walk down the path, away from him.

It was 18 months before she had further contact with Gareth, answering the phone one day to hear his dulcet tones. 'Lisa, I am calling to let you know that Gramps had a massive heart attack and died.' Hearing those words, she broke down and cried. 'I hate asking this of you, but can you be with me at the funeral? Please, Gramps loved you, as did Nana,' he pleaded.

'Of course I will, I loved them both.'

The funeral was as grand an affair as Nana's, the mourners paying their respects in droves, the church bursting at the seams. Lisa knew that this was the last of Gareth's blood relatives, in his mind, and that he would need her at his side to help him through the day. As Gareth read his eulogy, holding tight onto Lisa's hand for reassurance, he could see a figure at the back of the church that made his blood run cold. Lisa saw his whole demeanour change as he took a step forward to confront the woman he hated most in the world.

Lisa, having seen his mother, squeezed his hand, whispering, 'Carry on sweetheart, ignore her.'

Ann Edwards had seen the change on her sons face and bolted for the door, afraid of the confrontation she feared was building. After the wake Lisa started to clear away the empty plates and glasses, Gareth trying to stop her.

'Look, you can't face this on your own, let's do it together,' she insisted. When the final pot was in the dishwasher, they sat side by side, talking about the funeral and the unwelcome visitor.

'I wanted to kill her,' Gareth recalled. Lisa wrapped her arms round him to drive away any thoughts of that nature. He sighed, melting into the arms he had longed for for so long.

Taking her by the hand. Gareth led her up the stairs to his room, pausing to ask, 'Are you ok with this?' his voice unsure.

Sensing his conflict, her smart mouth took over. 'Is the Pope Catholic?' she quipped, making him dissolve into laughter.

'I love your smart mouth, babe.'

They undressed each other with reverence, making love to each other's bodies, worshipping at the altar of carnality, touching, caressing, kissing, becoming one, feeling each other's needs, easing the longing that they had felt for each other. They dressed quietly and again she walked away, kissing him deeply, passionately; she left him behind.

Lisa's life was far from easy; she had to rely heavily on the help of babysitters to work the many jobs she needed to keep her head above water, receiving little or no help from John, who failed to keep up his maintenance payments for the girls. She had three horses to care for, which took time and considerable effort on her part: Lana, a thoroughbred cross Irish draft that she kept as her own riding horse, and Bonita and Duchess, Arab mares that she was breaking and schooling for customers. Lisa had been remiss in her training of her now unruly Doberman, Tarron, due to work commitments, so decided to make an effort and take him to the local dog training club at Walmer Bridge. It was at the club that Lisa met Bill Turner, the next mistake in her life and one that ushered in a dark period for her.

Bill Turner was in the business of selling pet foods and a regular visitor to the club, where they allowed him to sell his products. He seemed to be a personable man who was easy to talk to. After a couple of months, during one of their many conversations he mentioned that he needed a shop assistant, to which Lisa offered her services. Lisa started to work full time for him, making life far easier for her. The hours being nine am until four pm enabled her to go to the horses before and after work. Her wages for this one job outstripped all the other jobs combined, and with the money from her horse work she managed to make ends meet.

Lisa had been heading toward the shop to begin work when she spotted Gareth on the main street. Pulling over, she climbed out of the car and hugged Gareth, much to his delight. Spending a few minutes to catch up, she told him that she had a new job at the pet shop. He didn't seem surprised, yet promised to start buying feed for his animals there. Gareth was well aware that Lisa had started a new job and of where it was located, knowing every detail about who owned it. He made it his business to know every facet of Lisa's daily life, including those people she mixed with. If she could not be with him, he needed to protect her.

Bill proved to be, on the surface, a caring, generous man, offering his help in every aspect of Lisa's life. He had a troubled home life, with a domineering father and bullying brothers who tried to interfere in his business. He was enamoured of Lisa, drawn to her vulnerability, homing in on her naivety and insecurity, her trusting nature allowing him easy access into her life. She proved to be a hard-working asset to his business. He found her a sympathetic, understanding ear and opened up to her regarding his family. It came as no surprise then when he broke down to Lisa, saying that he had been kicked out of the family home. She immediately offered him a place in her spare room as a lodger, the extra money coming in handy when the mortgage was due. Bill moved into the spare room and proved to be a great help. He was an average looking man with aquiline features and dark curly hair who made Lisa laugh; they got on well. Lisa soon started to warm to this kind man and after 18 months their relationship changed, Bill moving into her bed. Lisa was totally unaware that after her split from Gareth he had followed her everywhere, always at a distance; what Lisa took to be chance meetings on the main street were anything but. He knew her daily routine inside out and was well aware that Bill Turner had moved into Lisa's home. The thought of that oaf sharing Lisa's home drove him to distraction.

Nana Baxter had left a sizable legacy in her will for Gareth, amounting to 100,000 pounds. Gramps Baxter had left him the farmhouse and land where he had spent the happiest times of his young life, plus a further ninety thousand. Adding to that, his legal practices had taken off, proving most successful. Many of his stepfather's clients followed in his wake, his reputation preceding him. His teams were the top legal minds around, their reputations drawing in clients for all aspects of legal work. He decided to diversify to make his money work for him, having heard of a business investment that would give him an in road to the leisure industry. The night club in Liverpool was in need of renovation, going for a knocked down price in a prime location. He snapped it up and sent a top team in to complete the renovation, overseeing every aspect himself. He needed to keep busy to take his mind from thoughts of Lisa. Why did she not want to be with him? What was wrong with him? How did he not compare with the oaf that she was with? Such thoughts were self-destructive, leading him to lose control, and he could not have that. He did not want to go on without Lisa in his life, but had made a solemn promise to her that he would always be there for her should she need him.

Lisa had always believed that she would never be good enough for Gareth and still thought that way. She took it for granted that a man from his background looking as he did, a wealthy businessman, would have beautiful women throwing themselves at him in droves; why would he want to be with her, taking on all her baggage? She was partially right – he did have beautiful women trying to attract his attention ever present, but to no avail; he only had eyes for her, his one and only true love. Women that pushed themselves at him lived to regret their boldness, their advances rejected in the cruellest manner, leaving many of those opinionated madams believing him to be gay; after all, how could he possibly resist them?

Bill Turner's demeanour began to change after six months in Lisa's bed, almost as if he could no longer keep up the façade. It started with him picking at things that she had done, finding fault with the least little thing, jealous of the fact that Gareth would come to the shop to buy dog food once a fortnight and would engage in open shows of affection. The changes became more cruel, Bill's true narcissistic personality showing itself. He had chosen Lisa for her looks and the fact that he found her easily manipulated and, later, intimidated. His plan was to make her increasingly more dependent on him, knowing how much her girls meant to her proving an asset to his plan. He did less and less around the home, becoming fat and lazy. After the final battle with his family, he abandoned the pet food business, taking a job at the local dairy. Lisa would always find ways of making money, again taking on several part-time jobs, plus the monies she earned from the horses. It soon became evident that Bill could not work with others, unable to take orders as he deemed others below him. His true belligerent, argumentative self came well and truly to the fore. Bill started to pull Lisa down, just as John Metcalf had done before him, gleaning from it a feeling of power over her that satisfied his self-important, narcissistic ego. Lisa had always stood firmly in Bill's corner when it came to his family and the business that he left behind, backing him 100 percent. Bill, however, failed to return the favour when his father started to verbally attack Lisa, accusing her of splitting their family apart. This caused tension between them that eventually lead to an argument, resulting in Bill packing his bags and moving back into his family home, much to his parents' dismay.

Lisa was in a blind panic; how would she manage without him with two girls? She steeled herself and set about finding an extra job to take up the shortfall.

Lisa had always worked extra hard to provide for her girls, as the men in her life seemed to absent themselves from their responsibilities. She had just managed to get home from her job at the nursing home, the latest of her part-time efforts to keep the cash flowing, when the phone rang. On answering it she heard a voice that made her heart leap into her throat.

'Lisa, I need you, Jake is dead.' Gareth's unmistakable tone sobbed.

She gasped. 'Oh dear God, what happened?'

Catching his breath, he said, 'The vet is just leaving, he had a twisted gut, please come.'

In a second she was in her car, driving towards his home at speed, tears streaming down her face. As she drove into the stable yard at the back of the property, she could see Jake's dead body with Gareth cradling the magnificent animal's head, hunched over him sobbing. This horse had held fond memories of his Nana and Lisa, holding them close while he lived. As she approached Gareth looked up. Still kneeling, he turned as she stroked his head. He wrapped his arm around her waist, burying his head into her body. He let his heart break and they cried a river for the loss of the mighty animal that had given them so much, making their own bond stronger.

Finally cried out, Lisa summoned up the energy to ask, 'What happened?'

Gareth replied, trying to regain his composure, 'The vet operated but the gut was impacted with grass cuttings. When I checked the paddock, some idiot had tipped grass from their lawn over into the field. The vet said it had caused so much damage he would not recover, so I let him go. Please stay with me, Lisa, I have a man coming to bury him here and I don't want to be alone.'

'I have to get back to the girls, but I can stay for a while.'

They sat and reminisced about the happy times they had with Jake. Lisa could see Gareth relax as his recalled their time together out riding, not a care in the world, just the rhythm of shod hooves on concrete as they laughed, basking in their love. They stood and watched the grave being dug but, neither being able to bear the thought of watching Jake's body being lowered into the darkness, they walked away having said their goodbyes.

Lisa made her way home having made a solemn promise to Gareth that she would return. She made sure that her girls were with their father and his parents, returning to Gareth as quickly as humanly possible. He was waiting for her, having chilled a bottle of wine, and told her that he would prepare them something to eat later, that he wanted to celebrate Jake's life. He had placed a screen up against the wall and a projector to watch films that he had made of Jake. As they watched the majestic animal being put through his paces he broke down and sobbed, his heart breaking at the loss. Lisa wrapped her arms around him, and they melted into each other's caress. He needed Lisa to heal his breaking heart, needed to feel her touch, to be held deep inside her in the only place that gave him comfort. She knew what he needed, what they both needed, yet sensed that he was holding back.

In her usual smart-mouthed manner she said, 'Well, are you going to take me to bed or not?' He took her by the hand and led her upstairs, his heart skipping a beat, all doubt washed away. He undressed her with reverence, worshipping at her altar, making love to her slowly, tenderly, savouring every touch, every kiss, covering every inch of her body. Their bodies melded together as one; this was as fate intended.

He eased himself into the deep warmth of her moist sex, slowly building up momentum, wanting this to last forever, but unable to stem the tide of his desire, as his orgasm overwhelmed him he cried out, 'Dear God help me!'

Lisa exploded. Her body had ached to feel his power, the feeling of being complete, being one as he pushed deep inside her, filling her, easing her emptiness. They wrapped around each other, savouring every second, knowing that it could be their last. 'Stay with me babe, please, you have nothing to back for, I will look after you and the girls,' he pleaded.

Lisa's insecurities came flooding back. She did not want people to think that she was a gold digger. This beautiful man could have his pick of the beauties that mixed easily in his circles, where she felt like a fish out of water. She could not be what she thought he wanted, when the truth of the matter was that she was everything that his heart desired, his one and only soulmate. She kissed him tenderly, knowing that she loved him but resigned to the fact that she could not be with him. The thought of being a kept woman was something that her fiercely independent nature could not stomach, and she would not give anyone the opportunity to brand her a gold digger, a lesson she learned at the hands of his parents.

The following morning they said their goodbyes. Gareth kissed her deeply, passionately; her whole being cried out for his touch, yet she had to go. Her girls would be home soon.

She walked through the front door of her home and immediately knew something was not right. To her dismay, Bill had moved back into her home in her absence. He had found life back with his family far from easy, being relegated to the bottom of the food chain yet again. At least with Lisa he was king of all he surveyed, and he needed to be back on top. He spun Lisa the yarn that he had missed her and was lost without her, that he would turn over a new leaf. He was very convincing when his back was against the wall. Lisa was taken in by his outpouring and decided to give him a second chance, although in truth that decision had been taken out of her hands, as he had already made the move back; he was not leaving anything to chance. His only thought was of himself, a true narcissist in every sense of the word. His change of demeanour was short-lived. Being unable to maintain the façade, he reverted to type, picking at the least little things that Lisa did, putting her down about her appearance. Lisa regretted her decision but was unable to summon up the courage to do anything about it; after all, she had her girls' wellbeing to think about. Their home life needed to be stable and nurturing. Lisa hated trouble and upset of any description. Her empathic nature suffered greatly, dragging her down to the depths, reducing her to tears, and Bill knew exactly how to make that work in his favour.

Lisa loved Christmas, it was always a special time for her and the girls, yet Bill went out of his way to make it as miserable as possible. Christmas held no joy for him, and that was all that he was concerned with. After a tense Christmas Day, Lisa got the girls ready for bed. Their father was collecting them to take them to their grandparents'; they would spend the night and have another Christmas Day on Boxing Day. As Lisa waved them off, she was content in the knowledge that they hadn't missed out on anything because of Bill's attitude, but he was spoiling for a fight. As soon as she entered the house, he started on about the mess the girls had left and how the meal left much to be desired. Her heart sank, and in that moment she wondered how Gareth was. When Bill didn't get the required response from Lisa he flew into a rage and stormed out of the house, thinking he was wounding her by leaving her alone on Christmas night. Little did he know that on Christmas Eve she had received a phone call from Gareth, who was not feeling too good. He was alone and had not coped well with any of the tragedies that had befallen his life; yet again he told Lisa how he missed her.

Alone, she decided to find out how he was, and on hearing his voice it was evident that things were not good. On replacing the handset, she grabbed her car keys. Rushing to her car, she sped her way to the farm, where Gareth was waiting. He had heard her vehicle pull onto the gravel drive; he ran to meet her as she climbed out of the car. He grabbed her, lifting her from the ground. She instinctively wrapped her legs around his waist, immediately feeling the steel of his erection against her sex; this was as natural to her as breathing. He carried her into the house, elated that she was by his side once again to heal his pain. He poured her a Southern Comfort and lemonade, her preferred tipple, and himself an expensive single malt. His eyes never left her face – he gloried in the perfection of her eyes, her mouth, her lips, the way her face lit up as she animatedly recounted the girls' opening their presents, how Tarron had helped them, ripping up the wrapping paper to confetti size bits, and how the house was filled with laughter that seemed to annoy Bill greatly, the mention of his name causing Gareth to scowl, his lips tightening white. Lisa was drinking to forget the terrible mistakes that she had made in her life and the pain they had caused her. Here she sat with the most beautiful man that she had ever known, a man who adored her; he could give her everything that she needed and more, yet his position and wealth, the very things that would allow him to do that, acted as a barrier.

She looked into his azure blue eyes and there it was, that bewitching smile that she could not resist. Leaning forward, he cupped her face in his hands as he tasted her lips gently, tentatively. She needed to forget, to lose herself in his touch. She kissed him back hard, forcing her tongue into his mouth, biting his bottom lip. His eyes wide with desire, they were lost in a frenzy, tearing at each other's clothing, ripping buttons from their threads. His desire had been bottled up for longer that he could remember, and he needed to let his passion flow freely. Tearing open her shirt, he bared her breasts, sucking at her hardened nipples as she tore at his waistband. In a second, they were naked, Gareth scooping her up. Lisa instinctively wrapped her legs around his waist as he rammed his steel hard erection into her pouting sex with such force she cried out. Pressing her up against the lounge wall he pushed harder, deeper, biting her neck and shoulder as she clung to him. He could feel the ache in the pit of his gut building.

Turning, he pulled her closer and threw her onto the couch. 'Turn over,' he commanded. She turned face down and he grabbed the back of her hair, pulling it, forcing her up onto a kneeling position. Again powering into her cleft, now dripping with desire, he forced himself deeper as she gasped and moaned. Reaching round her thigh, his fingers seeking out her engorged clitoris and rubbing frantically, he could feel her orgasm begin to spasm against his cock, its urgency driving him on. Pumping harder, faster into her, he could contain himself no longer. She reached between her legs, grabbing his balls, and squeezed as he filled her with the molten heat of his seed. They cried out as their orgasms washed over them in unison. They lay with beads of sweat covering their flushed skin.

He wasn't done with her yet; scooping her up from where she lay, he cradled her in his arms as he carried up the stairs to his bedroom, tenderly placing her on his bed. He kissed her forehead, her eyelids, her nose, and her mouth, sucking, tasting every morsel. He worked his way down her torso, licking the pearls of sweat that formed on her breasts and stomach. Pushing her legs apart, he buried his head between them as he pushed his fingers into her still pulsing sex to find her g-spot. He stroked the tender flesh, keeping time as he tongued, sucked and nipped at the swollen bud of her clitoris, the sensation driving her wild as she felt her second orgasm begin to tighten. Lisa grabbed his hair and, pulling him up her body towards her, she rolled him over onto his back, straddling him. His erection began to harden in response to her juicy sex being rubbed up and down its length, massaging it into its hardened state. She impaled herself on its rigid length, pushing herself up onto a squatting position, her feet on the bed. She rose until the tip barely touched the outside of her turgid flesh and, smiling, she dropped, letting the full weight of her body freefall onto the sensitive organ, plunging it deeper and harder than ever before, making him shout. She continued to rise and fall until she felt her own need begin to take over her body, and reaching behind her she squeezed his balls as he exploded into her depths. She slumped forward, her head on his chest. Kissing the top of her head, he relished the fact that her naked breasts were pushed close to his chest and he was still deep inside her. This was where he was happiest, a place of comfort connected to his one and only. They lay together until the morning light filtered through the curtains that veiled their love from the world.

Lisa woke with the tingling feeling of arousal. As she looked down the bed, Gareth had his head between her legs, licking and sucking her clitoris, fingers of one hand stroking her g-spot. He lifted his head and, beaming, wished her good morning, promptly going back to the matter at hand, working his tongue hard against the tender bud until he heard her moan and felt her moist flesh tighten around his fingers, her release taking her breath away. Satiated, she felt the need to shower. Hungrily, he watched her naked body wend its way to the shower room. In a trice he joined her under the flow of the water, his steel hard member nudging at the globes of her bottom. He cupped her breasts, rolling her nipples between his thumbs and forefingers. Throwing her head back against his shoulder, she moaned, turning to face him. He lifted her from the ground. As she wrapped her legs firmly around him, he leant one arm against the wall, the other holding her up, his erection finding its mark as he pushed up into her pulsing sex. He powered into her, undiminished by the events of the previous evening. He could never get enough of her; he wanted to be inside her skin, to possess her mind, body and soul for eternity. This was his heaven, his reason for being put on this earth, he believed, to be her protector, her guardian above all others. They dried each other and dressed, laughing at Lisa's aching head due to her overindulgence in Southern Comfort, and ate a light breakfast.

'I have to get back to Tarron, I only arranged for a sitter to let him out this morning.' Her voice shaking, she knew that they could not keep doing this. Gareth pulled her to him and held her close, kissing her gently. They parted, his heart heavy as he watched her drive away from him once more.

Lisa spent the remainder of Boxing Day with Tarron. She needed time to quiet her mind. The girls would not be back until later, so walking with her beautiful Dobermann in the park helped to clear her thoughts, no one pulling her down, no one tugging at her heartstrings, no one demanding her time; she was free for a fleeting moment. Bill Turner had spent Boxing Day at his twin brother's home but made his way back to Lisa's where, yet again, he threw himself on her mercy, knowing full well that he could manipulate his way back in. He fooled Lisa before, he could do it again, and her good heart allowed him back as always. She decided to drown her sorrows – that was the only way that she could stomach Bill touching her. She found sex with him an unpleasant chore and was grateful that it lasted only a matter of minutes. This had escaped Bill's attention, as he was only interested in his own gratification, merely rolling over and falling into a deep sleep, his loud snoring reverberating around the room.

The holiday period over, Lisa was back into her work routine, the girls back at school. Her daily struggle to make ends meet was never ending. Her birthday came round very quickly, and she intended to numb the whole proceedings with a liberal amount of alcohol. After bedding the horses down for the evening, she headed home via the off licence, laden with four cans of special brew, a bottle of Southern Comfort, and the obligatory bottle of lemonade. When everyone was fed and the washing up done, she sat with a can and watched the television, switching off to the world around her.

She hardly heard the phone ring; jumping up, she lifted the handset. Perfectly spoken dulcet tones floated over the line. 'Happy birthday, babe!' Gareth gushed.

Her heart leapt. 'Aw, thank you sweetheart!'

They chatted away, laughing, unaware that Bill was eavesdropping from the kitchen. As they finished their conversation, Bill could contain himself no longer. Pouncing, he shouted, 'Oh, your boyfriend still in touch, is he?' His face and double chins angrily reddened, lips pouting like a cod fish, a term his father often used to humiliate him. Gareth had caught the beginning of Bill's outburst, and asked Lisa to put him on. She held the phone out to Bill, who flatly refused to talk to him. Lisa said her goodbyes and turned to face Bill, who had disappeared into the kitchen. Nothing else was mentioned. Lisa resumed her evening tipple until she fell asleep.

The following morning there was an envelope on the mat behind the door addressed to Lisa. On opening it she found a beautiful birthday card from Gareth, containing 200 pounds in crisp 20-pound notes. There was also a note that said, 'Buy a little something for yourself babe.' Tears welled up in her eyes; he knew she was struggling, and this was a king's ransom to her. Worlds apart, she mused, Bill had not even bought her a birthday card let alone a gift of such magnitude – he had been hard pressed to wish her many happy returns. This set the standard for the rest of their relationship.

The following week, Lisa felt a familiar churning in her gut that filled her with dread. Heading to the chemist, she bought a pregnancy test kit and, rushing home, carried out the test, the results of which filled her with self-loathing and horror; it was positive.

She was in a daze when the phone rang. Hearing the cultured voice say, 'How are you, my sweetheart?' she dissolved in a torrent of tears. 'Whoa whoa, what on earth is wrong babe?'

As Lisa gave Gareth her news, he felt his world crumble beneath him. His only thought being, how could she make a go of it with that loathsome individual? Trying to cover the dismay in his voice, he asked how she felt about the pregnancy. Hearing that she was distraught, gutted, that she made Bill take precautions that had obviously failed, did nothing to ease the breaking of his heart. They finished their conversation telling each other how much they missed and loved each other, while their hearts shattered again into a million shards.

Gareth put the handset down, unable to catch his breath. He felt as if he was freefalling, any control that he had dissolved at the sound of the words 'I'm pregnant.' He slumped in a chair. Throwing his head back, he screamed. God, how he needed to wipe it all away, he couldn't bear this feeling. His tortured soul wanted to end the pain once and for all, yet he had made a promise to protect her. He retrieved a bottle of good single malt from his drinks cabinet, drinking half down in one go. Not satisfied by the results, he finished the whole bottle, going in search of a second and third until he laid comatose on the lounge floor.

Ray and Steve knocked and found the door open, which was unusual. They didn't know how long he had been laying there and had only called round on the off chance that they would catch him, as he hadn't put in an appearance at any of his businesses. Gareth's Dobermann Ben greeted them in an agitated manner, dashing backwards into the lounge and returning to them as if to show them what was amiss. As they reached the door, they could see Gareth's body lying on the floor face down, the aroma of whiskey filling the fetid air.

Ray knelt and, on touching his body, exclaimed, 'Christ man, he is cold to the touch!' Steve quickly joined him and together, turning Gareth over, they could see that he had vomited and was choking. They lifted him onto the couch and quickly set to work reviving him. Smelling salts waved several times under his nose brought him back to consciousness. Hoisting him between them, they dragged his upright body round and round the lounge until he made an attempt to take steps on his own, promptly throwing up into the bargain. They dragged his sorry self up to the shower room and, sitting him on the tiled floor in the corner, they turned the shower head on cold, blasting full force over his body.

Springing into action, he grabbed Steve, pinning him up against the wall. 'What the fuck do you think you're doing?' he bellowed.

Ray grabbed the arm that he could see was cutting off Steve's air supply. 'Gareth, Gareth, come on man, we're trying to help you!'

Looking at Ray through the haze, he calmed down, and slumping to the floor he vomited again. They dragged him back under the water, turning it to a gentle heat, and left him propped up there as they went to clean away the mess he had left behind him. Poor Ben had soiled the carpet and was greatly relieved to be allowed out.

'Look at that, the poor dog can't have been out in days. Christ knows how long he has been in that state. This has to be Lisa again, she is the only one that could make him lose it in this way.'

Steve's comment rang true to Ray, who went and put the coffee on. 'He is going to need plenty of this,' he chuckled.

It was an hour later when Gareth made an appearance. Looking decidedly sheepish, he apologised for his behaviour and thanked them for their efforts in cleaning away his mess. He felt remorse for his beloved Ben's suffering, yet overjoyed when the big lad bounced all over him, relieved that his dad was back with him. Gareth's love of the breed came from Lisa, another connection to her now that Jake had gone, having purchased him after Lisa had introduced Tarron to him. He was taken by the breed's clean line and unfailing loyalty.

It had come to Gareth's attention that two Russian guys had been asking questions at his club in Liverpool, trying to find out where he lived. It seemed that they were in some way connected to the diplomat's son who Gareth had crippled during a match fight some time back. Apparently, unable to cope with the nature of his injuries, he had committed suicide, provoking his father to employ the two men to seek out the man he held responsible for his son's demise. Loyal to a fault, Gareth's handpicked staff were not forthcoming with the information they needed, forcing the men to return to the club at a time when the man himself would be able to meet them on his own turf. He had employed an ex-police officer called John Scully, whose career had ended abruptly when he beat his duty sergeant to a pulp after finding out that he was interfering with little girls. A bouncer at the club, Gareth had found him to be what he described as a 'handy lad.' John's nickname was Bull, and with good reason. Standing at six foot three and built like his nickname suggested, the muscular mountain of a man was a formidable presence. Gareth decided to employ Bull as his own private security man, offering him accommodation at the farm.

Ray and Steve were duly notified that Gareth would be making an impromptu visit to the club and that he may be in need of their help. No questions asked, they followed him to the club in their own vehicles. Gareth arrived at the club to be met by Bull, who had already been briefed about the Russians. He had given the bar staff notice to finish early to make sure that the club was clear. They hadn't turned up as yet, but had been seen in the area, so were expected. When they finally arrived, they entered the club individually some 15 minutes apart, going to different parts of the club after ordering drinks. They were unaware that they were being watched. As the club's clientele began to thin, closing time drawing near, the bar staff made themselves scarce. Gareth emerged from the office behind the bar, flanked by Ray and Steve. Bull, who had been on the door, came in, closing the inner doors behind him. The two Russians stood, shouting a warning in their native tongue that they believed the men facing them were armed. Gareth, being fluent in Russian, assured them that they were indeed armed and wanted to know the reason for their visit. They were taken aback that this man could speak Russian like a native, informing him that he was responsible for the suicide of a Russian diplomat's son, having inflicted injuries that he never recovered from during a match between the United Kingdom and Russia. It was obvious to Gareth where this was going, and he did not intend to waste any more time. Drawing from the shoulder holster inside his jacket with lightning speed he fired the Colt, silencer already in place. The gun hissed its report as two shots fired, hitting their mark in the centre of each of the men's foreheads. They dropped before they could fully draw their own weapons. Bull checked both the bodies, removing all items that could identify them; rings, watches, car keys, passports, and weapons. Gareth had bought a disused airfield locally, a secluded spot that proved to come in very handy in the months to come.

'Bull, get rid of them at the airfield.' Gareth instructed. Steve and Ray assisted Bull as they loaded the prone forms into the plastic-lined boot of a 5 Series BMW. Bull handed the keys for the club to Gareth and left immediately, leaving Steve and Ray to look at the CCTV footage and alter it accordingly. It appeared that the Russians had made the whole trip in their own vehicle, so that too was taken to the airfield, where all identifying marks would be etched out with acid. It would then be taken to a remote spot and burned out.

Steve and Ray were shocked at the swift actions that Gareth displayed that evening. Although they deemed them necessary, they were becoming increasingly worried as his whole demeanour hardened, taking no prisoners, rolling over anyone who dared to challenge him or block his progress in business, some of his businesses leaning decidedly towards the criminal element. His reputation as a man not to be trifled with was quickly spreading through both his legal work and business circles. He consolidated the name of Mr. Fix It, being the go-to guy when your back was against the wall – his services commanded a high price.

Gareth was impressed with the ease that Bull showed when dealing with any situation, being equal to most tasks, always the consummate professional when the situation most needed it. It was then that Gareth decided that he would build a security force second to none, the deciding factor being a break in at the club which cost him dearly, the perpetrators of which were found by Bull and dealt with summarily. Gareth recruited trained men when possible, ex-soldiers and those with top martial arts skills. He demanded that they be physically fit and drug free; to that end, he arranged for them to have full, state of the art physical examinations that he called their 'MOT' every six months. Those found to have gained weight were given a fortnight to lose it or lose their jobs; if tested positive for drugs they were instantly dismissed. They were kitted out with Armani suits, the cut of which accommodated the larger muscular form and hid any holstered side arm that they were also required to carry. Always dressed in shirts and ties, under which they all wore Kevlar torso vests, the required footwear was calf-length leather boots, made to carry knives and a smaller calibre gun. Gareth made sure that they were inspected and briefed before undertaking any job. He provided each with a BMW or Audi saloon car with blacked out windows. He believed image was paramount and made sure that they kept the rigorous standards that he required. Gareth demanded loyalty and respect from his men, and in return he helped them and their families find suitable housing and paid them royally. All were schooled by him in the martial arts initially to assess their capabilities. If they fell short, they were given over to an instructor, who made sure they were honed to perfection. He ran all the men that worked for him with the precision of an army commander. He always led by example, pushing himself to extremes in the gym that he had built onto the side of the farmhouse, along with a swimming pool. Everything was geared up to aid optimum physical fitness. He valued those who worked for him, more so those that now lived with him, although he always remained apart, aloof, watching.

Steve decided to seek out Lisa to ask for her intervention, as Gareth's leisure pursuits had become increasingly more dangerous. While his promise prevented him from ending his pain, he did his utmost to help fate succeed where he could not. Base jumping, freefall skydiving, rally driving, pushing the limits of speed and risk, becoming the ultimate adrenaline junkie; anything to mask the hurt that haunted him daily. He took Bull bungy jumping just to experience the rush of plummeting towards the earth at speed. Unfortunately, Bull failed to keep his eyes closed, and he bellowed all the way down, spending the following weeks with bloodshot eyes that resembled those of a white ferret.

After the skydiving he promptly announced, 'If you want to kill yourself, do it on your own, that is me done.' Although, recanting, he undertook a trip to the Grand Canyon with Gareth, Steve, and Ray, base jumping from lofty heights, being the last to jump into oblivion he decided that he would rather go for a drink, leaving a hastily written note pinned under a rock at the site where the others had jumped from and hopefully, he mused, would return to. The wind speed had picked up, blowing the flimsy paper away down into the depths of the canyons. The group were in a panic as Bull had failed to land and a search party was immediately dispatched to find him. As the light failed, they returned to the leisure centre and hotel that organised the various pursuits, agreeing to resume the search in the morning but not holding out much hope of finding him alive.

As they entered the building, they could hear Bull's voice booming out from the bar lounge. 'That took you some time, lads,' he beamed.

The look of astonishment and disbelief on their faces said it all. Gareth was furious yet mightily relieved. 'We've been looking for you, that is why we're late, you idiot.' With his usual devil-may-care attitude, Bull informed them that he had left them a note at the jump site – what more did they need? Bull's antics were to keep Gareth amused and perplexed in equal amounts during their long association.

Steve watched and waited until Bill Turner left for work one morning, making his way to Lisa's home. She was pleasantly surprised to see Steve at her door. 'What is wrong Steve, come in.' She tried to hide the feeling of foreboding that slowly crept over her.

'I need to talk to you about Gareth, love, I am afraid he is not coping too well. Would you please come and talk to him? He is taking unnecessary risks with his life because you are absent from it.' His plea was heart felt.

'Steve, I can't keep going there, it is crippling me, and he must have someone else in his life by now, surely?'

Steve shook his head. 'That won't ever happen, you have to know that by now. Please think on it, he really needs you.' He hugged her, leaving her stood at the door, knowing that he had failed to convince her, yet he wasn't for giving up; he would get one of the others to intervene.

Bull was the next candidate to visit Lisa, and a bit of a shock, as they had never met before. During his short visit he became besotted with Lisa, yet another moth to the flame. He too left a lasting impression on Lisa, as she found him easy and funny to be with. He lifted her spirits but failed to convince her to reconnect with Gareth. Her heart just would not stand seeing him, touching him, all he would need to do is smile that smile and she would be lost.

After 21 hours in labour, Lisa's baby son was born, and for a short while Bill became the doting father – at least when there were outsiders present, following in the footstep of his predecessor. To Lisa, the atmosphere at home was tense, not a place for a baby to be settled into. She likened it to a powder keg. Bill picked at everything she did, putting her down at every available opportunity. Baby Edward was five months old when Bill had reached the end of his tolerance. Lisa's post-natal depression was getting on his nerves; the baby and his mother were taking the spotlight from him and that was unforgivable. He picked his moment to unleash his venom, spouting his disapproval until he reduced Lisa to tears. He pushed her towards the front door, placing a bottle of paracetamol onto her hand, and opening the door he pushed her out.

'Here, go and kill yourself with these if you feel so bad.'

Lisa was barefoot, distraught and had nowhere to go. She made her way round to the home of a friend that regularly babysat for her. She was welcomed in and given a warm drink to steady her nerves, waiting for the woman's husband to return home. Lisa was assured that he would walk her home and see her safely inside, as she was in a panic that the baby was home alone with Bill.

When Lisa was escorted home, Bill answered the door, only to be asked what the hell was going on. He sheepishly backed down, being the bully boy that he was, a yellow streak a mile wide when it came to dealing with his own sex. Lisa thanked her escort and assured him that she would be ok. She was subjected to three days of total silence, being sent to Coventry, totally ignored. Bill's infantile behaviour suited her fine, as she was feeling fragile to say the least and had no tolerance for upset. She needed the place to be peaceful for baby Edward to settle into his routine. Lisa's home life was deteriorating, the constant put downs from Bill taking its toll. He had started to gain weight, taking on the appearance of an angry bull hippo, while Lisa lost far too much weight, her ribs and spine becoming prominent. The weight lost was so pronounced that even from afar Gareth spotted her alarming appearance. He needed to speak to her and find out what was going on in her life that had such a profound effect on her physically. He had always followed her at a distance and at different times until he had her routine down, knowing exactly where she would be at any given time, barring accidents. He was loath to contact her, as she had seemed to be getting on with her life and he had no wish to cause her any problems, but this was serious.

Waiting until he knew she would be home, he rang. 'Hiya babe,' he beamed as she lifted the handset.

Her heart skipped a beat at the mere sound of his voice. 'Hello sweetheart,' she gushed.

'I am a little concerned about something, can I come and see you?' he enquired.

'I don't think that would be a good idea, Bill will be home and a visit from you would cause problems,' she offered, the strain in her voice evident.

'Then come and have a little lunch with me, just for a chat, a catch up.' How could she refuse him? she thought, agreeing.

She changed baby Edward, making up a formula to take with her, along with extra nappies. Loading the car, she set off to the farm. He met her on the drive as she got out of the car. He wrapped his arms around her, giving her a long awaited hug, which should have been the sweetest of moments as she held him close, yet it filled his heart with dread, as he could feel that she was a shadow of her former self.

'My god, girl, you have lost a lot of weight,' he commented, hiding his concern.

Releasing her, he walked round the car and lifted baby Edward in his carry cot from the front seat. He remarked that it wasn't very safe having the cot on the seat that way and that he had seen her struggling with the cot as he had driven past her on the high street. To her amazement, he had bought her a proper baby seat for the car to make sure the baby was safe at all times when travelling. As they entered the farmhouse, Bull greeted and hugged her. Gareth instructed him to give them time alone, which he promptly did, no questions asked. The table was set, and they ate their meal, chatting as if they had never been apart. Gareth noticed that rather than eating the meal he had prepared, she was moving the food artfully around the plate, very little actually going into her mouth.

'You haven't eaten much, Lisa, you really should.' She could hear the genuine concern in his voice, not something that she was conditioned to hear as all Bill did was try and destroy her self-worth to make himself feel better. She smiled sweetly and admitted that she really didn't have much of an appetite. She felt at ease with him and watched with adoring eyes as he amused baby Edward, feeding him his bottle and changing him. What a natural he was with babies, she mused, recalling how he was with both the girls, smiling at the happier times in her life. They spent a wonderful afternoon chatting about their times together and the direction that Lisa's life had taken. Not once did they touch on what had been happening in Gareth's life and for good reason, although she did manage to pluck up the courage to ask if he had found himself a lady to love, to which she received an emphatic 'No.' Hugging each other like their lives depended on it, they said their farewells. That would be the last time that she would see him for quite some time, although he would contact her by phone from time to time and also shadowed her from a distance without her knowledge. Arriving home, she unpacked the baby's bag to find an envelope from Gareth containing 500 pounds, causing her to dissolve in tears. He always took care of her.

Lisa had made a promise to Gareth that she would take better care of herself. As the post-natal depression was taking its toll and conventional medicines offered no release, a friend told her of a homeopath that had worked wonders for her, so Lisa made an appointment to visit Kate Austin, who proved to be a godsend. Her remedies took care of the depression in double-time, amazing Lisa and piquing her interest in the workings of homeopathy. She found out that she would need the sciences before being accepted onto a university programme that covered homeopathy. Not prepared to give up at the first hurdle, she enrolled in and open university program that enabled her to work from home, and within 12 months she had obtained the science grades needed to enrol in a full-time course at Lancashire University. Bill was far from happy at this turn in Lisa's life and made it as difficult as possible, commenting that she would never stick to it.

She soon got into a routine of rising at 4:30 in the morning to turn the horses out on the 17-acre plot of land that she recently rented for a nominal sum. The land was closer to home, allowing her to spend far less time travelling and enabling her to get to university in time for the start of her lectures. She was determined to complete the Bachelor of Science course, which spanned a three-year period, having already completed a year with the open university. Along with keeping her family fed and clothed and managing her home, plus keeping the horses in tip top order, she would study hard into the early hours, getting no help whatsoever from the leech that was Bill Turner, who only gave her 130 pounds a month, keeping the bulk of his pay packed to himself. As difficult as he made her daily routine, she would match his efforts with renewed determination, having to obtain a student loan to continue, which only served to anger Turner further.

All the while, Gareth observed from a distance. He knew exactly which course Lisa was attending and her daily routine; he marvelled at her strength and determination, knowing what Turner was doing, having overheard him bragging about her having to give up soon due to him withholding funds. From that time on, Gareth made sure that every eight weeks he would post an envelope containing 200 pounds through her door, simply saying For Lisa Only. With the money that Turner was hoarding he bought himself a Land Rover, his pride and joy, buying parts to tweak the vehicle and make it faster. Gareth was so enraged by the lowlife's treatment of Lisa that he had his own Range Rover Sports fitted with a state-of-the-art Bull bar and grill guard, following Turner from Lisa's home one morning at a safe distance so as not to arouse suspicion. He had taken a road that he knew would intersect with the road being travelled by Turner and waited at the junction. As Turner's Land Rover drew level with the junction, Gareth floored the accelerator, powering the heavy vehicle forward, hitting the driver's side door of Turner's vehicle and pushing it off the road. Reversing, he floored the accelerator once again – he was going to make sure there was nothing left for the lowlife to recover. Turner was visibly shaken and could not recall seeing the face of the man driving, who had a baseball cap pulled down over his face, and the side windows were heavily tinted. All Turner saw was a smile on the face of the man as he drove away. Of course, the police were unable to trace the vehicle. Gareth had left nothing to chance, fitting a set of ghost plates. In spite of all Turner's best efforts, Lisa passed her course with honours. On the occasion of her graduation, she saw no reason to attend, having obtained the all-important certification. All the rest was just window dressing in her eyes, but Gareth attended, hoping to spend time with her to celebrate her achievement against all odds, yet finding her absent from the proceeding. They were so alike in many respects; he too had graduated with top honours from Cambridge, in spite of his stepfather withdrawing his funding, gaining a scholarship. She was the glove that fit his hand, when would she ever realise that? He would wait an eternity if that's what it took.

Lisa was oblivious to the fact that Gareth was ever present, in the shadows, watching, keeping her from harm's way. She had accepted her life with Turner, his investment in the home upkeep always kept to a minimum. She found ways to supplement her income while she built her client base up, her expertise being spread by word of mouth. She made teddy bears, her attention to detail being appreciated by a local toy shop owner, who ordered a regular supply from her. She also proved to be a talented artist of equine caricatures. Always able to generate cash, she would never be beaten down, yet still filled with dread at the thought of Turner withdrawing the pittance he gave her, she endured his foul aggressive narcissistic personality.

It had now been many years since she had seen Gareth face to face, although he would ring from time to time to hear her voice, checking on her wellbeing. She had no idea of the life that he had been leading or the reputation that he had earned as a gun-for-hire or the man who could steal any prestige car made, having relieved a noted celebrity of his Bugatti Veyron, a car that was supposed to be unstealable, according to the manufacturers, merely because it was a challenge. He had built his empire on his reputation as a no-holds-barred businessman and someone not to be trifled with, his personality becoming increasingly more explosive and violent with the passage of time. His own men knew not to overstep the mark, as he would order them into the gym and show them why he was feared. He dealt with any angst between his men in the same manner, no fighting amongst each other was allowed outside the gym. Only under the strictest rules governing martial arts were they allowed to settle their differences. Any new recruits that fell afoul of his humour learned a lesson they never forgot. Gareth's control was the one thing that held him together, and he increasingly felt that without Lisa in his life he was losing his grip. He needed to gain back his control and to better understand Lisa's motives for distancing herself from him. His heart was broken and all the hurt that he had suffered in his life was rising to the surface, boiling his blood. He had to gain control.

He applied to the Shaolin Monastery in Dengfeng County, Henan Province, China to join their school of Buddhism and fighting in order to better learn control of self and to perfect his fighting skills. Given his grade, the highest available in the United Kingdom, plus his unbeaten record in the ring, he was granted admission to a life that would take him away from all he knew for 15 months. Having made arrangements for his business ventures to be taken care by Steve, Ray and Bull, he embarked on the journey that would prove to be a turning point in his life. On arrival at the sanctuary, he was greeted by an initiate who took him to his quarters, a basic cell containing a single bed, a table, chair, and raffia mat for meditation – no Western luxuries here. He was to meet their spiritual leader within the hour, a meeting that served to annoy Gareth, as the Elder Master merely sat and stared at him for what seemed an age without speaking. He felt as if he was under a spotlight of disapproval. When he finally spoke, the Elder Master asked Gareth in broken English why he had asked for admittance to the temple. Gareth explained that he was losing control of himself and was hitting out. The Master told him that his childhood was dark, leading him down the wrong path, and that the love of his chosen should be fought for and won back, if that was possible; if not, he must accept and walk away. Shaken by that revelation, as he had not given the Elder Master any information about himself, Gareth listened to the schedule of training that he would be undertaking in silence. The Elder Master was adamant that to further his skills, Kung Fu would enhance his fighting technique. At 4 am every morning the door of his cell was banged on, with the words 'Out in five minutes' being shouted. Gareth was always stood ready, dressed in his gi, which pleased the Master that had undertaken his fighting tuition. His tuition was on a one-to-one basis and proved to be the hardest graft that he had ever undertaken, pushing his mental and physical endurance to its very limits. At the end of almost every day his legs, feet, and fists would be bloodied and bruised. He was taught to perfect his balance, being made to stand on a single post five feet from the ground on one leg for prolonged periods, alternating legs until told to dismount. A large part of his tuition involved the use of what the monks called a Shaolin monkey stick, with which they performed elaborate gymnastic, almost balletic moves. They were required to balance on the slender pole, which was a formidable weapon in the trained hand. He was allotted chores that he must also undertake daily, involving grounds work, gardening, becoming part of the temple's community. At intervals the Elder Master would summon him to talk in depth about the spiritual aspects of the temple teachings and also to delve into Gareth's past life. The Elder Master told Gareth that the path that he had chosen was dangerous and would bring him nothing but emptiness and pain. To his astonishment, he talked about Lisa as if he knew her. He was schooled in the art of meditation and had to learn the Buddhist teachings, being given the six primary rules to learn by heart. He also perfected his writing and speaking of the Mandarin dialect. He was allowed one visit home during the 15 months to deal with a pressing business matter.

As Gareth finished his fighting tuition, he bowed in respect to his Master Instructor. In the time it took him to straighten up the Master had covered the ground between them, head-butting and kicking him. His face almost touching Gareth's, he stared deep into his eyes, waiting for a glimmer of reaction. As the rage filled Gareth's being, he breathed deeply, swallowing the volcanic reaction down, burying it in the pit of his gut. Still the Master waited to see if he was in control. After what seemed an age to Gareth, who stood fast, breathing deeply, the Master patted his shoulder. Stepping back, he bowed to Gareth, who had achieved the goal they required from him. At the end of the 15 months, Gareth had proved himself to the monks in every respect, gaining a sense of inner peace; they had kept their word, helping him to piece back his control. At his final assessment, when asked to recite the six primary rules he had been given and his understanding of them, he proved yet again that he deserved their faith in his abilities, granting him the title of Shaolin Master on the understanding that he must complete a further six months' training in the United Kingdom and return to be assessed by them.

Gareth's security firm gained the reputation of being second to none, rivalling those of the armed forces. Employed by the rich and famous, who valued his discretion, he also provided them with a club where they could relax unhindered by the general public. His hatred of drugs and those that dealt in them became legend. Those foolish enough to deal in any of his establishments would be made an example of in the harshest ways possible. Such shows of force became common place, alerting the local exponents of organised crime, who became annoyed at this incursion into their business dealings by this usurper on their territory. Thinking that they were merely dealing with a businessman who needed to be taught a lesson, they would dispatch a gang to teach him the errors of his ways and to obtain protection money or lose his properties.

One such incident involved the Chinese Triads operating out of Manchester's Chinatown. They were met by a force that they had never encountered before, headed by the man himself, who always fronted such meetings of the minds. Gareth had handpicked the men to accompany him on these occasions based on their unique skill sets, always flanked by Bull, Steve, and Ray. They had been tipped off that the Triads were on their way. Knowing the numbers involved, Gareth had assembled three Range Rover Sports and three BMW 5 Series, four bodies in each, comprised of his top men, all suited, booted, and armed. They timed their arrival just as their visitors were gathering in the carpark of the second of Gareth's clubs. What became his trademark entrance in years to come, the sight of the awesome Black motorcade arriving, doors opening, their lethal contents unfolding into plain sight, instilled fear into anyone witnessing the precision manoeuvre, as their athletic muscular forms all lined up, dressed to intimidate, all wearing black leather gloves. For the first time the Triads came up against a force that outclassed them when it came to the sheer magnitude of skill, precision, and violence. Gareth, at the head of the phalanx of highly trained assassins, always made the first move. Having heard enough of the threats issued by these pawns, he delivered a crippling blow with his fist, followed by a kick that silenced the mouthpiece forever. The skirmish that followed was over in a matter of minutes, one being left standing to return to his masters, to relay the message that this was no ordinary businessman and that he would not tolerate their products being peddled in his clubs or in any areas where he had businesses. In a clinical, professional manner, the scene of the mayhem was cleaned of its debris, ready for the club's clientele to arrive. All was as if it had not happened, the motorcade disappearing as quickly as it arrived.

The message was received with a mixture of fury and respect. The reply that came back from the Sun Yee On was that a meeting should take place between the two organisations to discuss an amicable solution. Gareth intended to expand his businesses into more areas; not wanting to have to continually battle for territory, he agreed to the meeting. The issues that were not open for discussion and a definite no in Gareth's books were drug trafficking, human trafficking, prostitution, and extortion. After a lengthy and awkward meeting, eased by the fact that Gareth could write and speak Mandarin, the Sun Yee On agreed to his terms, with a clause that they could call on each other should they require a show of strength in the face of other factions' incursions. This contract ushered in a long and peaceful association that was called on from time to time, cementing the relationship between the two organisations.

Gareth had retired to his bedroom, seeking peace and quiet from the noise reverberating from the bodies that seemed to fill his home of late, its walls filled with framed photographs of Lisa and Jake, her jodhpurs and T-shirts washed ironed and neatly folded in his dresser drawers as if she had never left, the perfume that she used, Charlie Red, in his bedside unit, sprayed nightly on the adjacent pillow, which he held close as a reminder of her body lying in his arms. Everywhere was a reminder, a shrine to his chosen one.

He could hear Bull bellowing from the gym as he pitted his prowess against Ray and Steve on the treadmills when his mobile phone pinged, alerting him to the arrival of a text message. Scanning the display, his heart leapt; he recognised the number, it was Lisa's mobile. Should he answer? What if it was that cretin she lived with? His mind in turmoil, reading the text his face lit up with a smile that illuminated the room. It read, 'Hiya, it's me, I suppose a shag is out of the question?'

Laughing out loud, he concluded, 'Yes, that's my girl.' 'Where and when?' was his quick reply. She asked him to ring her later and hoped that he wasn't with anyone, to which his reply was just as quick: 'You are the only one for me and always will be.' He was like a teenager with butterflies in his stomach, excited at the prospect of hearing her voice once again.

Lisa's life had been blighted of late, culminating in a house fire that resulted in her and Bill, along with her three Dobermanns, living in a caravan on a 14-acre plot of agricultural land that she had bought from a friend. Also living on the land in a static caravan was the woman who had bred Lisa's three dogs, along with her own dogs. Bill was working late, and Lisa was feeling low. Being cooped up with Bill in such a small space was taking its toll, yet she knew there was a light at the end of the tunnel; the work on her house would be completed in eight months, or so she had been promised.

Lisa had become firm friends with Jackie Smales, their love of all animals, especially dogs, making a strong bond. She had invited Jackie for a drink while Bill was out. They sat around the table, laughing and joking, Lisa becoming increasingly more intoxicated as the evening wore on. Her tongue loosened by the effect of the drink, she summoned up enough courage to mention Gareth to Jackie, who had an innate dislike of Bill, having seen his behaviour and treatment of Lisa firsthand. Jackie told Lisa to contact Gareth. What could she lose? She could not understand why Lisa had not mentioned him before, he seemed so right for her. Feeling the effects of the Dutch courage she had liberally imbibed, she started to text Gareth, telling Jackie what she had written, causing her to choke on her drink, roaring with laughter.

'Well, it's not the best chat up line in the world, but very succinct and to the point,' she chortled.

Lisa had told Jackie that she was going to meet Gareth the following evening but not what time. As Jackie checked her kennel dogs were settled and comfortable for the night, she spotted Lisa weaving her way unsteadily towards the five-bar gate at the front of the property. Smiling to herself, Jackie thought, 'Good on ya gal, been hitting the Dutch courage again I see.' Taking out her mobile phone, she started to play the theme tune to Mission Impossible, which was her ring tone, as she watched Lisa trying to climb the gate, nearly hanging herself with the shoulder bag she had slung round her, only to be told to 'Shhhh fuck off Bill is asleep!' at the top of her voice, reducing Jackie to hysterics as she watched her drop to the ground and weave her way down the road to the lay-by below the Italian restaurant where Gareth was waiting in anticipation.

He watched, smiling, as she wove her way towards him. Not convinced that she would cover the full distance upright, he set off running towards her, only to be jumped at and knocked backwards as she launched herself at him. 'Fancy meeting you here,' she giggled, sending him in to spasms of hysterical laughter. He ushered her towards his BMW, opening the front passenger door as she opened the back.

'Oh, are you not riding up front with me?' he asked tentatively as she flopped onto her back on the rear seat, pulling him on top of her, giggling loudly.

Neither of them had seen the couple walking from the restaurant toward them and were startled when a male voice enquired, 'Are you alright, love, do you need help?'

'Oh, I am fine,' she replied, still giggling uncontrollably. Gareth managed to break her grip on his shirt long enough to assure the couple that she was a little worse for wear. Pulling her into the upright position, he placed her in the front seat and fastened her seatbelt, only to be grabbed again. 'I've missed you.' She smiled lovingly at him, melting his heart and making him smile at the same time.

Climbing into the driver's seat, he turned towards her and asked, 'Where would you like to go?'

'Why, with you of course, silly,' she gushed. God, how he had missed her smart mouthed witty comebacks, the sound of her lilting laughter and her broad Lancashire twang. He was almost lightheaded with the elation of having his beautiful muse back at his side.

On the journey back to the Nana Baxter's farm she asked, 'What's wrong with you, then?' Quizzically, he shook his head. 'You usually put my hand on your mate down there,' she said, gesturing towards his groin.

Grinning from ear to ear, he took her hand and placed it on his growing erection. 'I didn't want to seem presumptuous,' he laughed. He smiled, remembering the many journeys in their past with her hand firmly in place on his erection; when she had queried the reason for him placing her hand there, he quipped, 'It's just in case we have an accident.'

He remembered her saying, 'That won't stop us having an accident.'

'No, but I will die happy,' he replied, giggling like a schoolboy. Looking at each other, they burst into fits of laughter like teenagers out on a date. It was just as if nothing had changed, yet life had changed them both in very different ways. Lisa was concerned that he would not find her as alluring as he had her younger self; she had gained weight, having lost heart with her life and being too busy taking care of others to take care of herself. How wrong could she be? He only saw his chosen one, the only woman that he needed. On arrival at Nana Baxter's farm, he lifted her from her seat and carried her into the lounge. She watched as he unbuttoned his shirt and marvelled at how his body had developed. Much time and effort had been spent on honing the body that stood before her, only serving to make her feelings of inadequacy grow. Holding up her hand, she stopped him as he stood there semi-naked, muscular, ripped, twice the size he had been when they had last been together.

'I am embarrassed to get undressed, I have gained weight,' Lisa said, her voice trembling. Lifting her chin, he pulled her close, and cupping her face in his hands he kissed her with all the passion and longing that 16 years had kept buried inside. Undressing her slowly, he kissed every inch of bare flesh, telling her how beautiful she was, her trepidation beginning to melt. As he lifted her from the floor as if light as a feather, he climbed the stair cradling her in his arms, his precious one. 'I am too heavy–' she started to say, but he pressed his finger to her lips.

'Shhh,' he whispered, and laying her gently on the bed he removed the rest of his clothes. Kissing the full length of her body, starting at her head, he worked his way down, worshipping her, making love to the woman he had needed for so long. Every time he reached a part of her body that gave her cause for concern, she made to stop him, only to be told 'Shhh, you are beautiful.'

It had been so long since she had been touched in this way, since her body had been adored and caressed. She was lightheaded at his touch. He gently pushed her legs apart, kissing her inner thigh and dipping his tongue into her pouting, juicy cleft, searching out her clitoris, sucking and stroking. Revelling in her moaning as he pushed his finger inside her, stroking her g-spot, he felt her body begin to tremble as her orgasm built. Reaching out to his bedside unit to retrieve protection, she stayed his hand.

'Not necessary,' she said, 'I have been sterilised.'

'Of course. I don't think they would be any good, they are very old.' The relief on his face was evident; how he hated using the damn things. Lisa relished the feel of his tight, hard body pressed against her fingers stroking and kissing his chest as he pushed himself into the one place he knew he belonged, the only place he found comfort. He made love as he had never made love to her before, pushing himself deeper into her, moving urgently, building momentum, filling every inch of her being. Whole again, he powered on until their orgasm ripped through their bodies as they melted into each other's arms. He had made her feel like the only woman in the world, and she was, in his mind. He had never had eyes for anyone else and never would. As they gloried in the afterglow of their love, wrapped around each other, she stroked his muscular torso, marvelling at every inch of his perfect definition feasting her eyes on a body that had changed so much with the passing of time that she hardly recognised it. He was simply magnificent.

Pushing him away and rolling him onto his back, he could see the wicked glint in her eyes as she mounted him, impaling herself on his erection. 'How can you be ready again in such a short space of time?' she asked with a girlish smile.

'I have waited a long time imagining this moment, the mere touch of your hand makes me ready,' he smiled, that smile she had missed so much, the smile that got him anything he wanted.

'I have missed you, big boy.' Her smart mouth brought a blush to his cheeks. 'Let's see how ready you are.' Rising to her feet, knees bent, drawing his penis out until only the tip remained inside her, she started a rising trot, dropping her body down its length with force and rising again, the power of the drop forcing him deeper, making him cry out in ecstasy. She rode him hard with no let up until he burst inside her, the force of his orgasm pushing her over the edge. Both exhausted, they surrendered to the kiss of Morpheus, sleeping bodies entwined.

Lisa woke with a start, feeling alive and wanting more, yet knowing that she had to return to her life before Bill rose for work. He gazed into her eyes. 'Is this a one off, Lisa?' he enquired, not wanting to push her, believing his previous insistence had driven her away.

'No, I want to see more of you,' she replied with such conviction his heart leapt for joy in his chest. They showered, luxuriating in each other's touch. Lisa's spirits soared, elated that he had not judged her, making her feel desirable and loved. It was as if they had never been apart, being with him was the most natural thing in the world.

Returning Lisa to the farm gate, all was quiet. It was 5:30 am, there was not a soul stirring; even Jackie's kennel dogs were still abed. Turning to her, he kissed her deeply and asked when he would see her again. 'Today,' she gushed, beaming at him. As he watched her climb the five-bar gate and drop down onto the farm driveway, giggling as she tripped, he laughed. God, how he loved her.

He remembered very little of the journey back home, his head replaying every precious moment of their reunion, barely believing it wasn't a dream. Walking through the door and down the steps, he threw his car key into the bowl on the entrance hall table. The place was eerily quiet, deserted as ordered, the noisy bodies that usually shattered the peace within having been told to make themselves scarce. Sitting down, he sighed and buried his head in his hands. He sobbed, overwhelmed by the realization that she was back in his life, filling the debilitating gaping wound of emptiness that she left when she broke his heart. He was whole again, she completed him, he would not lose her again, of that he would make sure.

Lisa was giddy with anticipation. She couldn't wait for their meeting at 5 pm; not even Bill's sour-faced bad temper could knock her down today, which served to annoy him beyond belief. He was only happy when he had dropped her spirits and had her grovelling. Telling Bill that she was going to her mother's to see Edward, who was staying there while their home was rebuilt, the one place that she knew he would not venture near as he hated her mother with a passion, a feeling that she returned with interest. She drove to Gareth's home to be met on the drive by Gareth, Bull, and Ray. Opening the door for her, Gareth helped her out of the car, only to be lifted off the ground by Bull, who hugged her so tightly that she could not breathe.

'Hello, darling, we have missed you!' he bellowed. She laughed, thinking that there was nothing understated about Bull, a larger-than-life presence. She hugged him back. Ray waited patiently to give the lady that had made their lives so much easier with her return a hug. What a beautiful man, she thought as Bull dropped her to the floor and Ray wrapped his arm around her, kissing her lightly on the cheek. He had flawless, richly tanned skin and dark brown, sultry Mediterranean eyes. All of them seemed to have grown in stature. The years that had passed had been more than kind to them; like fine wines they had improved, belying their years. Just as quickly as she arrived Gareth guided her to his car to whisk her away.

'Where are we going?' she questioned.

'It's a surprise,' he said, smiling.

She caught her breath as they pulled up outside Honeysuckle Cottage. All their memories came flooding back; the heavenly scent floated through the air, greeting and welcoming them back to where it all began.

'I didn't think that you would still have this place after all this time,' she said, looking quizzically at him.

'How could I let this go? It holds everything we were within its walls.' He pondered wistfully for a second before getting out of the car and walking round to open her door for her and unfasten her seat belt.

'I can do it myself, you know,' she laughed, taken aback by his attentive actions.

'It's my pleasure, babe,' he said, flashing the smile that instantly melted her heart all over again.

Walking through the door into the cottage brought back many bittersweet memories. He closed the door as she took in the scene before her. He had filled every room with exquisite blooms: lilies, her favourite, and roses of every hue. Not one surface was without a scented candle burning brightly, filling the air with a sensual aroma. The table had been set, with attention to every detail. He had lovingly prepared a vegetarian meal for them, ready to be served at a minute's notice, yet Lisa had other ideas. No need for Dutch courage today, she followed him through to the lounge, decked with garlands of flowers of every type. As he turned to face her, she hit him mid-chest, knocking him down flat onto the couch, diving on top of him.

'Right, tiger, let's see what you're made of,' she growled, tearing at the buttons of his shirt, sending them flying across the room. His face lit up as he saw the wicked glint in her eyes. They rolled onto the floor, stripping their clothes off. She mounted him, impaling herself on his steel-hard erection, riding him so hard he cried out in exquisite pain. His cries fell on deaf ears as she rode through the same pain, oblivious as their volcanic eruption ripped through their bodies, collapsing on top of him, totally spent. Beads of sweat glistened on their bodies.

He kissed the top of her head and with all the ease of a big cat pushed himself upright, lifting her with him. He cradled her in his arms as he took the stairs two at a time. Entering the bedroom, the smell of roses hit her; the bed and floor were covered in a carpet of rose petals. Gareth had covered all the bases in the art of seduction in the most lavish manner possible, all to please his one and only. He intended to make up for 16 years of lost time and longing. He dropped her onto the bed, making her giggle, and immediately rolled her over face down. Grabbing the back of her hair, he pulled her head back, his hand between her legs, lifting her to her knees. He bit hard into the flesh of her firm, round buttocks, making her yelp, his fingers probing her succulent quim, searching out her swollen clitoris. She moaned as he stroked and pressed the engorged nub, the sound that jumpstarted his erection, making it so rigid it was painful, and the only way to ease the ache was to plunge it deep inside the body he has yearned for over and over again. He powered into her, taking her breath away, still tender from her erotic ride. She pushed back against his muscular, flat stomach, their bodies melding into one. She grabbed frantically at the bedding as he yanked hard on her hair, pulling her head back, forcing himself deeper, harder, relentlessly until they exploded together, collapsing into each other's embrace.

'You really did miss me then,' she gasped, trying to catch her breath. God, how he loved her smart mouth. Grinning from ear to ear, he looked deeply into her eyes and merely nodded. He wined and dined her, reminiscing about all the times they had spent there, in the place where it all began. The time flew past, heralding her time to leave and go back to her makeshift home. Gareth dropped her at the farm gate, kissing her deeply, overjoyed that she had arranged to meet up with him the following day. Lisa floated down the drive to the caravan, counting down the minutes until their next rendezvous. Bill did not look up from his mobile phone when she entered; in fact, it was an hour later that he asked what there was to eat. Lisa was taken aback at how easy it had been and how little she meant to Bill, his mobile phone having become the new love of his life. For that she was grateful.

On the journey back to his home Gareth's heart was filled with joy, replete in every sense of the word. He resolved never to let her distance herself again, no matter what. Later that evening his mobile phone rang. The number on the display was that of one of his men working as internal security at a club in Manchester. He listened in horror as he was told that a young half-caste man called Lennie working as door security at the club had been raped by a group of three West Indian men. Apparently the three men had been asked to leave due to rowdy behaviour, so in order to placate Lennie and show him there was no hard feelings, they bought him a drink that they had spiked with the date rape drug. Finally leaving, they waited in an alleyway at the side of the club, intending to make the pretty boy pay for his disrespect, unaware that there were CCTV cameras operating out of sight there. As Lennie left for home, feeling a little worse for wear, they ambushed him, taking it in turns to rape him and, beating him to a pulp, they left him in the gutter. Gareth's security man had locked up and was on his way to his vehicle when he found Lennie's prone body. Gareth saw red and instructed his man to unlock the club and take the lad inside to try and bring him round, that he would be there in 40 minutes. Gareth, Bull, Steve and Ray climbed into one of a fleet of Range Rover Sports and sped off to Manchester.

On their arrival, Gareth instructed Bull to get copies of the CCTV footage while he spoke to the lad. His stomach turned at seeing the state of the lad, who was awake enough to tell them in no uncertain terms that he was not going to hospital. As they watched the footage from the cameras, their fury evident, Gareth's man identified each of the men involved, and he knew where they lived. Securing the club for a second time, Gareth instructed his man to take Lennie to Nana Baxter's farm, that he had arranged for a doctor to be there to deal with his injuries and check him out for internal damage. With Bull driving, the four set off to the addresses that they had been given, each pulling on their black leather gloves before setting off. They caught up with the first of the three men, a large arrogant thug who, when questioned about his actions that evening, made the mistake of thinking Gareth's cultured, correctly spoken voice made him gay and voicing that opinion. The first punch shattered the man's jaw; the kick that followed knocked him, dazed, to the ground. In a second his pants were unzipped and lowered. Trying to get to his feet, a third blow hit home, splaying him yet again on the floor, his arms now pinioned by the weight of Bull and Ray's powerful grip. The pain that ripped through his body as he struggled, screaming and writhing, served to remind him of what he had done as Gareth's cutthroat razor, which he had tucked down his boot, cut through the flaccid flesh of his penis and testicles with surgical precision. He lay and watched as his genitals floated in a river of his own blood towards the drain and disappeared from sight, finally losing consciousness. Turning, without breaking a sweat, they walked back to their vehicle, Gareth phoning the ambulance service to attend the scene of devastation he had left behind yet again. Each man met with a similar fate, making sure that their genitals could not be retrieved and reattached. All were duly warned what would happen should they speak of that night to anyone.

Gareth wanted to know more about the lad that he had taken under his wing; the information that came back was not what he expected. The 19-year-old had lost his beautiful blonde mother at the age of 12, when his father had murdered her and attempted to murder the boy, being stopped by his uncle, who raised him until he became too ill to carry on. The lad had a bad life, and it didn't seem to be improving. Gareth decided to keep him with him until he was well and offer him a job. The doctor, a cardiac specialist who Gareth had procured a vehicle for, checked Little Lennie (as Bull called him) out and treated his wounds, informing Gareth that he was bruised internally but there was no tearing, and he would be sore yet ok. He seemed more concerned about the psychological effects that the lad may suffer once the drug that he had ingested had worn off and that he should be kept an eye on for any tell-tale signs. There were many occasions that warranted the attention of a medical specialist when using hospital A&E services would draw unnecessary and unwanted attention from the police. Gareth made sure that Lennie was settled and comfortable in one of the upstairs bedrooms, leaving him to sleep off the effects of his ordeal. Gareth was becoming increasingly more aware that his recent incursions into others' territories could bring consequences that, while not a problem to him or his lads, could prove problematic to his relationship with Lisa, and he could not allow that to happen. He had built up a security force second to none that covered Hull, Leeds, Preston, Manchester, Liverpool, Birmingham, and London, having thriving businesses in those areas, being sought out by organisers of major events ranging from pop concerts to Royal visits. Handpicked, he could call on any of these men at any time day or night, no questions asked. He was hard but fair and ran their units with military precision. They were paid the highest salaries with health insurance, and their families were taken care of; he expected in return their respect and loyalty. Many were ex-combatants, forsaken by the British Armed Forces, taken off the streets where they were living rough after being unable to integrate back into polite society due to their injuries, both physical and psychological. He helped them to piece their lives back together and gave them purpose and an outlet for their skills. No longer did they owe allegiance to the British flag but to the man who had given them their lives back, having been discarded by the country that trained them and used them up.

He resolved to sit Lisa down and explain to her the direction his life had taken in the years that they had been apart and forewarn her of the inherent dangers. How he would impart this revelation to her would take careful thought and consideration; he could only imagine how her smart mouth would react or if she would lash out. One thing he knew for sure was that she would not run away, and for that he was grateful. The events that followed made that decision a little redundant, to say the least.

He picked Lisa up from outside the farm gates, grinning from ear to ear as he watched her climb the five-bar gate to the property, beaming her smile as she successfully landed unscathed, which was no mean fete. They laughed and chatted, joyous at being back in one another's company again, making the journey to his home pass in a flash. Gareth had renewed the gravel drive leading up to his home so that no one could sneak up on the place. He pulled up outside the house and, walking round, he opened her door and undid her seatbelt, helping her out of the car, ever the gentleman. Bull and Ray were home and greeted her with a hug and a kiss, rushing off to the kitchen to make drinks for them all. They were sat chatting, catching up, when Bull stood up.

'Quiet,' he whispered, 'uninvited visitors.'

Gareth stood up, taking Lisa's hand. 'Sweetheart, please go into the kitchen.'

She could see by the look on his face that this was serious, and she immediately complied. Peeping round the corner, she watched as Gareth retrieved a sidearm from behind a book in his bureau. Bull tucked a second gun into the back of his jeans waistband as he walked to the door, flanked by Ray. There was a loud bang, shaking the door. A second bang caused the door to fly open, revealing three armed men. One immediately grabbed Ray, forcing him to the ground, his weapon against Ray's temple. Bull grabbed the second man, gaining a chokehold around his throat, his weapon pressing hard under the man's jaw.

The third man rushed in, weapon drawn, screaming 'Drop your weapons now or we will kill pretty boy here,' pointing to Ray. He had not seen the red dot on his forehead until Gareth moved the laser sight from his gun down the length of his body and back to the kill shot, causing him to drop his weapon. To his horror, he caught a movement out the corner of his eye as Lisa appeared from the kitchen.

'Leave the little lady alone, we will deal with her later,' instructed the only remaining armed assailant, as she walked in towards the back of the couch, tentatively feeling for the baseball bat that was always kept there. She sprang into action, launching herself at the man with the gun, hitting squarely on his head, knocking him down. Ray exploded with such ferocity the man didn't have time to recover, crumbling to the floor as his face disintegrated under the force of the blows that rained down on him. In a matter of minutes the incident was under control, the three intruders lying face down, weapons retrieved, their unconscious forms dragged unceremoniously to the back of a Range Rover – its boot was lined to prevent blood staining. This would be their last day on this earth, but no one would bear witness to that fact.

Ray wrapped his arms around Lisa, holding her close, and apologised. 'I owe you my life, you should not have witnessed that. He was going to kill me, he had nothing to lose.'

As the enormity of what she had just done dawned, her eyes filled with tears. Turning to Gareth, she fell into his arms and sobbed, the release of adrenaline overwhelming her.

'Sweetheart, I am so sorry that you had to witness that. I was going to talk to you tonight and give you an insight into the changes that have happened in your absence.' His words were heartfelt as her tearstained face looked up into his deep blue eyes adoringly.

'No time like the present, better late than never.' Her smart mouth relieving the tension, as always, he threw his head back and laughed out loud. Bull and Ray left them to chat as they set about the task of cleaning away the detritus in the back of the Range Rover. Lisa wanted to know the who and why of the matter. Having made her a chamomile tea to calm her down, Gareth sat facing her, hoping that what she was about to hear would not freak her out. He told her that he had wanted to die when she had left him, that he shed tears of despair daily, wanting to put an end to the pain, but that he had made her a solemn promise to always be there for her; that he had regularly taken risks with a view to leaving his fate firmly in the hands of the gods; that he had earned a reputation for being ruthless both inside and outside of the court room; and that as his business empire had expanded, he came into conflict with factions who considered him a threat to their own business ventures, usually those of a criminal nature. His dislike of drugs and any businesses involved in the manufacture and distribution of them would bring them into direct conflict with him, and he would make it his mission to end any such endeavours. He told her that he had become a gun-for-hire, undertaking contract wet work abroad on two occasions, both netting him in excess of three million pounds, and that he did his own research to verify that the contract targets were in fact deserving of the fate that they met. She questioned the term 'wet work' and was told the 'wet' meant blood. He assured her that he only dealt with vermin, the dregs of humanity, in that way and would never harm an innocent. He apologised as he explained that there would always be men that would come looking for him as he moved into new areas with his businesses, but that they would be dealt with in the same way that the men that had invaded his home tonight had been. He explained that her relationship with him would place her in the spotlight; he had effectively painted a target on her back, and she would need to have daily protection. If they could not get to him, they would seek to find someone he cared for in order to wound him, and he would not risk her life in that way. Lisa's eyes widened at his outpourings, hardly believing what she was hearing.

'Am I in a gangster movie? Am I going to wake up, is this a dream?' she questioned, pinching herself. Gareth at that moment wondered if all this may prove too much for her to take in and cause her to cut him out of her life again. 'How can you be a legal man meant to uphold the law and do all the things you have just told me about?'

Her troubled voice and expression prompted his quick reply. 'I felt nothing after you left me and felt I needed to push every limit possible. Most legal people bend the laws to suit their own purposes; I am no different, and I had reason to hit back at the system that failed me and the others that I employ. We all have an axe to grind against polite society and we use its own system and laws against it.' Her quizzical expression prompted him to reveal the one secret that he had buried deep in his consciousness, a secret that only one other knew. She listened in horror as he recounted the life of a little boy locked in a cupboard under the stairs at his parents' home, taken out, dressed to impress, and returned to his prison, only being taken out to go to his bedroom, where his mother systematically sexually abused him from the age of four up until the age of ten. Beaten by the man that hated him, ever the reminder of his wife's infidelity, locked away so that he didn't have to look at him. 'Dear God, why did you not tell me this before?' she gasped.

'I was frightened that you would see me as less of a man,' he admitted, voice dejected and eyes searching her face for some reaction. Her eyes filled with tears, and she pulled him to her. Holding him close, she sobbed for the little boy who had endured a sickening catalogue of abuse from the one person in his life he should have been able to trust, the one bond that should have been unbreakable: a mother's instinct to protect her young. He choked back his tears, trying to hide the tidal wave of emotions that welled up inside.

Knowing instinctively what he was feeling, she said in a whisper, 'Let it go, let it all go, it takes a strong man to show his pain.' They held each other close as he shook with the release of emotions that had been buried for almost 50 years. Holding him tightly, his head to her breast, her mind was working overtime piecing together the incidents from their past. It started to make sense; the reason he was a virgin at 23, being unable to stomach certain types of women; the reason that evil woman had tried to buy her off ... dear god, if he had only told her all her own insecurities would have appeared insignificant and they would have been together. She was filled with hatred for the people that had done this to him and cut to her core that he had not opened up to her, for all the time they had wasted when they could have been together. Gareth told her his so-called parents had divorced but that his step father had been diagnosed with cancer, a fitting end, she thought, for such a loathsome creature, his mother had moved back into his home to take care of him on the understanding that she be written back into his will, making her his sole beneficiary. The cold-hearted, calculating bitch always made sure she got what she wanted. Lisa wanted to kill her for her betrayal of her child and mothers everywhere.

They talked long into the night, almost forgetting that she had to go back to the farm. Life in the little caravan provided by the insurance company was almost at an end. For that she was grateful, as close proximity to Bill was unbearable to say the least. Gareth dropped her again at the gate to the property, marvelling at the sight of her climbing over and landing safely on the other side. Pulling away to start his journey home, he frowned, knowing that she was in danger because of their relationship. He resolved to put a security detail on her to shadow her throughout the times she was not with him. Gareth had suggested that they cycle together and, when he was at work, that his lads would accompany her to make sure she was safe.

His businesses in the local area had brought him into conflict with a large group of Pakistanis headed by an Imam. He had cost them millions of pounds of revenue to their drugs trade, and they intended to teach him a lesson. Their attempts to track him down to his home base had proven fruitless, but they had a lead on his lady, who would prove a worthy prize to taunt him with and draw him out. They intended to abduct her and make an example of the infidel bitch. They trailed her from her home on a daily basis, unaware that their every move was being monitored by a security force that waited in the shadows, the ultimate ambush predators. After weeks of trailing Lisa's every move, they struck. She had taken advantage of the beautiful sunny autumnal morning to cycle up the quiet country lanes that surrounded her home accompanied by Ian, one of Gareth's men. They were laughing and joking as they cycled side by side when a Steel Grey Audi RS4 cut in front of them, stopping abruptly. Two Pakistani males in their early 30s climbed from the vehicle as Lisa struggled to stay on her bike. Ian dismounted and walked towards them.

'Have you come to film us rape and torture this whore?' Their leader shouted at him.

'Yes,' he replied coolly, reaching into his bike frame pouch and taking out his phone and spring-loaded telescopic cosh. He quickly took a picture of the men stood by their car with the registration plates clearly visible, pressing the red panic button on his phone; it immediately relayed the images directly to Gareth. Ian pushed Lisa behind him and told her to stay there. In a daze, she complied without any argument. Ian opened the spring-loaded cosh with a flick of his wrists, hitting both men full on and knocking them to the ground. On seeing his cohorts hit the deck, the driver emerged from the vehicle, pointing a pistol first at Ian and then, to Ian's horror, at Lisa, who had been exposed as he had moved forward. With lightning fast reactions he hit the hand holding the pistol, knocking it to the ground, and flattened the driver against the car. As they struggled to stand, Ian rained a salvo of blows down on them just as two BMWs pulled up, two men in each. They collected the prone forms, bundling them into the boots of each vehicle, one of them remaining to drive away the assailants' vehicle; all evidence of the incident magically disappeared. Lisa was shaking from head to toe as the adrenaline coursed through her veins. This had made things very real for her, yet she was not going to be deterred from her daily routine by Asian thugs.

This would be the first of many attempts to take Lisa by this particular group of Asian thugs, who were funded by a wealthy Saudi who had lost many millions of pounds due to Gareth's intervention, and he was trying to wipe Gareth from the face of the earth, recruiting further Asians from London. Gareth, having done his homework, decided to systematically take out the sons of each family involved, making them disappear as if by magic. This served to throw the families involved into panic mode; their sons meant everything to them. Women were expendable, their daughters they would blithely throw away, but their sons' wellbeing was paramount. Gareth gave the order to take every young male over the age of 20 out of the equation to see what effect it had on Lisa's attackers, yet their Saudi master, although of the same ideology, would keep pushing them, regarding them as of a lower caste and expendable, money being the only God they worshipped. He had made it clear that if they could not find the man himself, they should play with his little lady before they finished her, and to video their efforts as a means of inciting the infidel that dared to interfere in their business. Gareth was beyond outraged when these words filtered down to him, having eyes and ears strategically placed within their organisations. The word came back that the Saudi would be joined at his prestigious hotel in London by two other Saudis, his partners in the drugs business, and that they would be there for a month before returning home, organising their drug businesses throughout the United Kingdom. Provoked into action, Gareth immediately handpicked the men to accompany him to London, briefing 20 of his men that lived and operated out of London to stand ready for his arrival. Three of them were instructed to book into the hotel at his expense, and to covertly monitor the comings and goings of the three Saudis at all times. They followed his instructions to the letter, though when the opportunity presented itself that afternoon, they tracked their quarry across London to an area where there were no CCTV cameras in operation. They took advantage of this error in the Saudis judgement. The three were no match for the onslaught that ensued, being ambushed and taken down by the three ex-marines. Taking the bodies miles away to a deserted woodland to be disposed of, they contacted Gareth and informed him that he had no need to make the journey with his men, that the matter had been resolved cleanly and efficiently. He was impressed and a little angry; he had wanted to inflict pain personally on the scum that had threatened his one and only. He trusted his men explicitly, and they were the top of their profession; he rewarded their initiative royally, yet he knew that the Saudis would not let go that easily.

The reconstruction work was finished, the decorators gone, the first of the new furniture was due to be delivered, starting with the king-sized bed needed to accommodate Bill's growing girth. Lisa was there to see the delivery men in and that the bed was placed correctly. Gareth joined her just as they left.

'Ooh, let's go buy some special bedding and christen this wonderful big bed.' And there it was, the smile that held the key to her heart. He adored shopping with Lisa, wanting to shower her with every possible gift he could, buying sumptuous bedding with which to christen the new bed, filling two criteria. As they left the shop, Gareth had a twinkle in his eyes.

'You know, I have never made love in a vehicle before.' Sounding almost crestfallen at the revelation, he looked with puppy dog eyes at Lisa.

She knew only too well what he was doing and, packing the boot with goodies, she replied, 'Let's take care of that then, shall we?' All his vehicles had blacked out glass in the back and rear side windows so, climbing into the back, they hurriedly removed each other's lower garments. Lowering the seats so that Gareth was laying back, Lisa mounted his steel-hard erection, grinning at the moan he released, the whole act heightened by the fact that busy shoppers were passing their vehicle on either side as they made their way back to their own vehicles. Gareth was becoming a shade too vocal, prompting Lisa to cover his mouth, giggling like a naughty schoolgirl. She rode him hard, bringing them both to their climax.

'That was such a rush,' he gushed, grinning from ear to ear, reminiscent of the Cheshire Cat. They dressed hurriedly and rushed back to make up the bed, which looked inviting, crisp and clean, just asking to be mussed up. The look he gave her was dripping with pure animal desire; he wanted to be the first to use this bed to make love to her, claiming her for his own and marking his territory. He prowled round the bed like a big cat stalking its prey. Pouncing, he tore at her clothes, while she unbuckled his belt, unzipping his trousers. In seconds they were naked. As he threw her onto the bed, he pushed her legs open, pushing his shoulders under them, kissing, nipping, sucking up her inner thigh. Licking her moist sex, his tongue pushing through her swollen lips, searching out her engorged clitoris. He tongued, licked, and sucked until he felt her start to shudder. He rolled her over face down and, pulling her up onto her knees, he grabbed the back of her hair as he rammed his steel hard erection deep into her velvet depths, making her cry out with the ferocity of his lunge. She had never known him to use so much force before, it excited her beyond belief as he powered on and on, digging his fingers into the flesh of her hips, smacking her rump hard, raking her back with his nails. She moaned and cried out as her orgasm ripped through her and he exploded in unison. Totally spent, they wrapped around each other until they regained their equilibrium.

'We really need to get dressed, Bill could turn up at any minute to see how the house is looking,' Lisa said, her voice sounding a little stressed. He complied with her wishes more for her than himself. He would like nothing more than to lock horns with the overweight slug of a man for his treatment of Lisa. He kissed her deeply as he left, crossing the road to his car just as Bill pulled into the drive in his van. He didn't care if he had seen him or not; in fact, he doubted that the oaf would even recognise him. Bill, ever wrapped up in his own dramas, walked into the place bellowing his doom and gloom, gesticulating as he regaled Lisa with the machinations of his working day. He had failed to notice Gareth's departure or the flush on Lisa's cheeks.

The house was fully furnished within the next couple of days and Lisa was ready to move back in, glad to see the back of the cramped conditions offered by the caravan, although she would miss Jackie's company. Having become firm friends during the time she had lived there, she had promised to visit Lisa daily.

Gareth had bought a second club in Liverpool and was interviewing men for the security duties there when one man in particular caught his eye, a powerfully built man with an impressive resume. He always undertook these interviews personally, as he had a very specific standard in mind that these men had to meet, and this one stood apart from the rest. Chris Broadbent was what Yorkshire folk would call 'a quiet club man', always blending into the background, watching, listening. He had been security for political figures and rock stars alike, known for not taking shit from anyone. He impressed Gareth, who was eager to see the man put through his paces in the gym. Chris did not disappoint. Gareth told him he wanted to see his body honed and cut within the next couple of weeks as he offered him the position. Chris was coming to the end of a relationship with a woman who had turned out to be bipolar and seriously psychotic, prone to attacking him in his sleep, resulting in him working two jobs that took him away from home. Bull had been sent with him to collect his belongings, resulting in the nightmare of a woman chasing them down the street, armed with a large kitchen knife.

His neighbour, watching the spectacle of two muscular security men running for their lives, shouted in hysterics, 'She is gaining on ya lads!' Chris had left his mobile phone behind, he informed Bull.

'Fuck it, I will buy you another,' he screamed, overtaking him as they ran to their vehicle to make a quick getaway. This was a story that they would never be able to live down, plaguing them at every gathering. Gareth laughed, shaking his head as they recounted their near-death experience – hardly the image he was looking for in his security team. He allotted Chris one of the bedrooms, which were now at a premium. He was going to have to do some remodelling of Nana Baxter's farm to accommodate his growing army. The once peaceful setting now echoed with Bull's bellowing voice, treadmills pounding, gym equipment clanging as heavy weights were pushed about daily. As the numbers grew, Lisa nicknamed the farm 'the Bull Pen', marvelling at the endless parade of semi-naked muscular masculine bodies that walked backward and forward to the gym and swimming pool through the lounge.

At the end of Gareth's long drive there was a single detached house that shared the first part of his drive. As numbers grew at the Bull Pen, given the nature of their work, there were comings and goings at all times of day and night, much to the chagrin of the occupants, an elderly couple who had been friendly with Nana. The house was proving too large for their needs, plus the added disruptions; with that in mind, Gareth came up with a solution to suit both parties, offering them way above the market price for the property, an offer they snapped up. Once emptied, cleaned, refurbished, and redecorated, no time was wasted moving Chris and Little Lennie out of the main house and into the 'Top House', as it became known, yet another deterrent to uninvited visitors.

Word had reached Gareth that a recently discharged soldier suffering with post-traumatic stress disorder, having served in Afghanistan, had come home to find that his wife had moved him and his belongings into the garage. He visited the address and found that the man was indeed living in a garage attached to the house. Offering him employment and a roof over his head, he moved Rick into the Top House on the understanding that he be seen by a specialist in post-traumatic stress disorder. Gareth knew that Rick was going to take more than most to pull together, as he was a little manic and on a hair trigger, yet his skill set could not be passed up on. During one of Lisa's visits, Rick took a fancy to her, making a comment about what he would like to do to her given half the chance – he had not known that Gareth was listening in the kitchen.

'Get out!' Gareth screamed as he entered the room. Rick, still new to the rules and regulations that he needed to adhere to in order to survive there, held his hands up and walked out, taking off on foot. Gareth had been making Lisa a drink when he heard Rick's loose-lipped comments. Handing her a drink and making sure that she was settled, he made his apologies, saying he would be back shortly, and left. Jumping into his car, he drove down the country lane from the Bull Pen; he had no idea how far Rick had gone in such a short time, but eventually caught up with him as he jogged towards the main road. Jumping from his vehicle, he grabbed hold of Rick, who exploded, lashing out wildly. Gareth's blows were precise and metered, disabling Rick, who would not go down.

'Don't ever disrespect my lady in that way again, or I will kill you.' Gareth spat, kicking Rick's jaw and breaking it, knocking him unconscious as he laid at the side of the road. Gareth called the ambulance service, telling them exactly where Rick was, and climbing back into his car he returned to the Bull Pen, cool, calm and collected. Lisa was oblivious to what had happened and that is how he wanted it to remain. Rick was very apologetic after his short stay in hospital, Bull collecting him the day he was discharged.

'A word to the wise, lad, show a little respect to Gareth and Lisa or it will end badly for you.' Bull's words were never to be taken lightly; as second in command, he was a force to be reckoned with. Gareth greeted Rick as if nothing had happened – as far as he was concerned the matter was finished. He accepted Rick's apologies, telling him he was to be on light duties until the wiring in his jaw was removed. Gareth was fully aware that with the type of men he employed, especially those that he had as his immediate security, those who shared his home, living in close proximity, that there would be angst and clashes of personality, and that he could not allow that sort of situation to develop, always sending those parties involved to the gym to slog it out under the watchful eye of Bull or himself. He needed to be sure that they would have one another's back when going into dangerous situations and not harbour resentment. If any showed disrespect to Gareth, he would take them into the gym and show them the errors of their ways, and that included Bull, Ray, and Steve. All graded exponents of the martial arts and, having the full measure of them all, he was their alpha, their boss, and always would be.

Lisa was back under her own roof once more, the fire being a close call, and according to the chief fire officer her guardian angel must have been working overtime that day, as something stopped the fire from ripping through her home and the house next door. Instead, it was confined to the lounge and kitchen where it started. Her relationship with Bill had diminished to that of landlady and lodger; she could no longer stomach any form of intimacy with him, his overbearing, belligerent demeanour and constant put downs to make himself feel superior taking their toll. Added to that, his expanding waistline and lack of personal hygiene plus his love affair with his mobile phone made him an abhorrent figure in her eyes. She had been shown that there was more to life than being someone's punching bag and that she deserved to be cherished and taken care of. Rekindling her relationship with Gareth revealed to her the shortcomings that she had endured in her past and present associations. Gareth made her feel like she was the only woman on earth, that she should be protected, lavished with all the comforts that his vast wealth could provide, yet the fiercely independent Lisa still carried with her the venomous words that his parents had spewed at her, and she was not having anyone say that she was a gold digger. Gareth had converted one of the downstairs lounges into a bedroom with French windows that looked out over the extensive lawns and gardens. They had chosen the decorations and soft furnishings between them, making it the retreat they needed from the chaos that shattered the shelter that the place once offered. This was theirs, and no one was allowed access unless invited. With a large flat screen on the wall, a chaise lounge, and one wall covered from floor to ceiling with state-of-the-art wardrobes and units that could be walked into, filled with clothes, Lisa was amazed at the finished room – and a little uneasy, as every available wall space was covered with framed photographs of her spanning every aspect of her life, along with portraits painted by the best artists money could buy. This pictorial account of her life spilled out into the main living accommodation; everywhere she glanced, her image stared back at her. In the drawers she found jodhpurs and tops from years ago, laundered and neatly folded, just as if she had never left. She found a bottle of Charlie Red perfume, the one she used to wear in her youth. Gareth told her that when she left him, he would spray the perfume on his pillows at night, as holding them close gave him comfort in her absence. The room was a shrine to her life and, if she was honest, the whole thing freaked her out. He had basically been her stalker for all the years that they had been apart, always in the shadows making sure that she was safe, watching her stumble through life, amazed that she had made it so far.

One thing that never changed was her love of life. Her empathic abilities honed with the passing of time, she had become an extremely knowledgeable and effective homeopath and herbalist, believing that the natural approach to health and wellbeing was the only way. Ever the magnet, Gareth's men were drawn to her warm, easy-going ways, making a beeline for her whenever she visited the Bull Pen, which was almost every night. Their room became a necessary haven from the growing number of Lisa's admirers.

Gareth had been contacted by a man from Galashiels in Scotland with information about a gang of Mancunian drug dealers, who had been driven out of Manchester by Gareth, setting up business in Galashiels. They had already been responsible for the death of one youngster and the serious condition of several others due to the product they were pushing in the area. The situation had become serious, local residents and police powerless to stop them. Gareth agreed to intervene, but wanted to know the background of the man calling for his help. Ian McDonald was 45 years old, a family man with two little boys. His boys meant the world to him; although his relationship with their mother had been over for some time, he stayed to take care of them. He feared for his boys' safety and did not want them growing up in an area that was deteriorating into a drug dealer's paradise. Ian was a body builder who specialized in nutrition and health, running what the locals call the 'fat club' at the local gym, which was one of three jobs that he held down to make ends meet. To earn extra money, he had become a cage fighter (no rules) and remained undefeated, taking on contenders from America and Russia. All these facts piqued Gareth's interest, yet he still needed to be sure that this was not a set up. Having gleaned all the information necessary from other sources, he arranged to meet up with 'Mac,' as Ian was known. The line of Black Range Rover Sports arrived at the gym where Mac worked. Gareth was impressed by the physique of the powerhouse that stood before him; climbing into the back of the vehicle, he seemed to fill all of the available space next to Ray. Gareth told him that the matter would be sorted but that he needed to go with them back to the Bull Pen, as he seemed to know quite a lot about their organisation and how to contact them and Gareth needed assurances that he was trustworthy. He had remained at the top of his field due to his caution, always covering every base when it came to the liberty of his men and himself. Mac wasn't happy but had little choice; he made two phone calls, making sure that his boys would be looked after in his absence. He was transferred to a second vehicle that would take him back to their base. The Mancunians underestimated the might that they were about to face, which lead to their demise. Their bodies were taken to common land outside of the area and burned, reminiscent of a tribal funeral pyre, which served as a warning. Mac was grateful that the problem had been sorted but was annoyed and worried that he was, in fact, a prisoner at the Bull Pen. Although he had all creature comforts, he needed to see his boys. Gareth was adamant that he stayed put but that he would give him a job and pay him a wage for the duration of his stay.

Lisa homed in on the newcomer's despair and decided to talk to him during one of her evening visits. Gareth had become accustomed to his lads seeking her out to help them with all manner of problems, mainly psychological, yet this man sat in a corner alone. Over time he began to open up to her about his life. Having been abandoned on the steps of a hospital at roughly the age of six days, not knowing his birthday or if he had any brother or sisters, his only family was his adopted brother Lennie and his two precious boys. The system had failed Mac and Lennie, passing them from one abusive foster home to another. Her heart went out to this colossus of a man, and she decided that she would ask Gareth to try and track down his family, if in fact there were any. No mean feat, yet he could see her genuine concern for this man's suffering, knowing that there would be more to her request than at first met the eye. While it took some weeks and the services of a firm of private investigators that Gareth employed for his legal work, it was found that Mac did in fact have family: three full brothers plus one half-sister and three half-brothers, the result of their father's dalliances. All eight offspring had been abandoned or given up for adoption, their parents being heroin addicts. Mac's full siblings all showed a strong desire to be united with their brother, while his half siblings declined the offer, not wanting disruption to their established lives; all but one, his half-sister, who had been waiting to track her family down for some time. Mac was overjoyed at the prospect of being united with them, no longer being the only one, and even more so when Lennie got back in touch. 'Big Lennie', as he became known, had been involved in the adult entertainment industry as a porn star for some years, making his fortune. He was keeping a watchful eye on Mac's boys in his absence, having contacted Mac by phone, elated at his brother's reconnection. Gareth promised Mac that he would work tirelessly at getting full custody of his two boys. It was then that Mac joined his organisation, becoming one of his top operatives; he never returned to Scotland. His boys joined him, the eldest was 11, the youngest being 9. Gareth paid to put them in the top school, and they never looked back.

As Gareth's organisation spread into other areas, those that he displaced sent out squads to track down the man who dared challenge their authority. It became a very real problem in that when they failed to track him down, as all leads petered out, they concentrated on finding someone whom he held dear; his one and only would prove to be the ultimate bargaining chip for them to use as they saw fit. Gareth made sure that once Bill left for work at 7 every morning. one of his top men would join her to help with her daily routine. while two cars with two heavily armed men in each watched the area for vehicles that looked out of place while constantly cruising the area, checking in at Lisa's home at intervals. Mac had been given the task of helping Lisa with her daily chores. She had told him that she needed to visit the local farm shop some ten miles away for provisions for the horses. Mac's brief was to follow close behind Lisa, making sure that she was not followed. Halfway to the farm store Lisa's mobile rang: it was Mac. He instructed her to pull onto the grass verge at the side of the road and wait. Moments later an Audi RS4 pulled onto the grass verge behind her, quickly followed by Mac in his Range Rover Sports. Mac had contacted Gareth, who was with Bull travelling towards Southport. He had been told where to stop and to wait for their arrival. Only one of the men alighted from the Audi, but made no move towards Lisa's vehicle as he watched the big guy in the Ranger Rover unfold onto the roadside. They wanted no witnesses to what they were about to do to the little lady, yet soon realised that this man was no member of Joe public. Gareth arrived with Bull, driving past Lisa's van and pulling onto the grass verge in front of it. The second of the two men had now exited the vehicle. As they watched Gareth climb out of his vehicle, pulling on his gloves, one of the men recognised the man walking towards them. Overcome by fear, he vomited at the roadside.

Lisa lowered her window and said, 'Aw, that poor man isn't well, please don't hurt him.' Gareth smiled at her innocence 'I am not going to touch him I just want to chat to him. Carry on your journey Mac will be with you'. He stood and watched as she pulled away followed by Mac. True to his word, he did not lay a finger on either of the men; that privilege was given to Bull, who made sure that was the last day they spent on earth. Gareth would not tolerate any threat, real or imagined, to his one and only. God help anyone who came close to harming one hair on her beautiful head; he would unleash Armageddon on those responsible.

Reaching their destination Lisa questioned Mac as to what would have happened to them. He informed her that they would have been made an example of to send a clear message to their bosses. When she said, 'Why? They were only following me,' he laughed at her naivety, telling her that they had not come to wish her well; quite the opposite. The reality, of which Gareth had once warned, dawned on her, making her feel sick to her stomach, yet this was the hand she had been dealt and had accepted.

Lisa had been reading about tantric sex and thought that it would be something different to bring to their relationship. Gareth bought supplies of Manuka honey and organic goat's milk from a local man who specialized in teaching tantric sex. Paul was a hippy by nature and all things natural and organic were his stock in trade. Gareth booked Paul and his wife to come to the Bull Pen to begin their lessons. The gym was clear for the evening and the lads were warned to keep away. Paul and his partner Liz arrived, lighting the candles that Gareth had purchased and arranged in the gym; they provided the only light and set the ambience for the lesson. Both were in their mid-50s with lean and toned bodies that belied their ages, having always followed the clean eating mantra of organic only and never eating anything that they had not prepared, processed food being a definite no-no. The first lessons covered the breathing and finding their centre, sitting on his lap, facing him, staring deeply into his eyes, breathing in unison. As they entered the gym, Lisa noticed that Liz had not taken her eyes from Gareth. Watching him closely, she seemed to be hypnotised by the way he moved. This had not gone unnoticed by Paul, who steered Liz towards Lisa to guide her through their initiation into the practices, while he concentrated on Gareth. Gareth had doubts at first, not being comfortable with another woman being present during his intimate connection with Lisa, yet appreciated that this would benefit them both in the long run. He could endure almost anything for Lisa; this, however, was right on the edge of his limitations. Lisa had forewarned Paul that Gareth could not tolerate another woman's touch due to his abusive childhood. Bearing this in mind, Liz showed Lisa how to touch his body, using Paul as her model. As they watched, Lisa could feel that Gareth was uncomfortable watching the intimacy of their touching. Squeezing his hand, Lisa smiled, seeing him immediately relax. This confident, ruthless Adonis of a man visibly sought out the touch of her hand to gain the necessary confidence to overcome a fear that made him physically sick to his stomach. The first lesson proved to be a daunting task for Gareth, but he could cope as long as Liz kept her distance from him and he had his muse there to help him deal with the intimacy the lessons required. Liz was fascinated by the man who moved like a big cat on the prowl, how balanced, perfectly honed and ripped his body was. A work of art in her eyes, one that she had not seen the likes of before. Her thoughts were far from those of the professional teacher that she was supposed to be. Lisa was acutely aware that Liz may prove to be a problem, her interest in Gareth making both Paul and Gareth uncomfortable.

They had arranged to have weekly lessons in the gym at Gareth's home in order to work towards their tantric masters' level, which would enable them, should they so wish, to teach others that were interested. Lisa was spending every available spare minute with Gareth, which was no mean feat. In fact, it was a logistical nightmare, fitting two lives into one.

Gareth had collected Lisa, taking her to the Bull Pen to have lunch with Bull and himself. It was a pleasant, sunny day, making eating lunch outside on the patio a pleasure, the beautifully landscaped gardens providing the perfect verdant back drop to their relaxing get together. As they concluded their meal, chatting, having a refreshing cold drink and discussing their day, a familiar and very unwelcome face appeared from around the corner of the house. Gareth had his back to the visitor, facing Lisa. Bull immediately rose to his feet and enquired if she had not heard of doorbells. The voice that answered caused the blood in Gareth's veins to freeze. Turning, he saw the face of the woman he despised most in the world: his mother.

'I am here to see my son, young man.' Ann barked.

Lisa could feel the blood boil in her veins. Standing, she let rip with every ounce of venom she possessed: 'How dare you show your face here, you deviant? You are a disgrace to motherhood, you sick bitch!'

Taking a step forward, Lisa felt a large arm encircle her waist and lift her effortlessly from the ground, hearing Bull's deep growl: 'Not worth it babe, let it go.' Lisa kicked against him to be released but he stuck fast, taking the brunt of her angst on his shins. Gareth was rooted to the spot, unable to move. He had erased her from his mind, it was a shock to once again see her, especially here, his one haven from her attentions.

'That is a complete and utter lie!' Ann raised her voice to meet the accusation, instantly aware of what Lisa meant. Lisa was now screaming in frustration as she struggled against Bull's grip to get free, aching to launch her attack on the abomination that faced her.

'I have told him to report your sickening attacks on him as a child to the police, it's about time everyone knew what a lowlife you are, and he has agreed!' Gareth, transfixed, merely nodded in compliance. How could she deny what she had done to him, calling him a liar? His mind was in turmoil.

'I won't be treated in this manner! I have merely come to inform Gareth that his father as died and that the funeral–'

Gareth, finally finding his voice, stopped her midsentence. 'I do not wish to know, he was not my father. Leave my property now or be removed.' The realisation that she was indeed about to be found out and her darkest secret made public caused her hurried departure from the property.

Bull finally dropped Lisa, his shins being black and blue from the kicking she had inflicted on him in her fury. Running into Gareth's arms, she could feel him shaking. Holding him tightly, she knew she had to defuse the situation. 'I would have had her if my feet had touched the ground,' she giggled, scowling at Bull. Gareth laughed at her wonderful smart mouth that always knew how to ease him out of tight corners.

Bull, rubbing his legs, looked up. 'Would not have looked good babe, she is 75.'

Gareth, still laughing, replied, 'I wouldn't have minded, we could have buried her in the woods.' Bull, rolling his eyes, hobbled off to administer first aid to his battered legs.

Ann tried on several occasions to catch Gareth on his own at the property, sick with worry that he would carry out the threat made by the woman she had tried to eradicate from his life for this very reason. Bull always managed to intercept her until in the end she realized it was a fool's errand. John Edwards, on his death bed, had instructed her to leave everything to her son to make amends for their abominable treatment of him, perhaps thinking that this last empty gesture would save him from the gates of hell.

The Bull Pen was buzzing; they had planned a surprise birthday party for Ray. All the lads were going to be in attendance. The patio and lawn were laid out with chairs and a large table containing all manner of delicacies, enough to feed an army of hungry menfolk. Bull, being in charge of the barbecue, had a mountain of organic fillet steaks, burgers, sausages, and chicken to preside over. Gareth, as usual, had footed the bill for the proceedings, always providing his lads with the best of everything. The bar was well-stocked, ready for the merrymaking to commence. Ray had been at the office all day; he was hot and sticky and in need of a shower. His face lit up hearing the lads all there singing Happy Birthday at the top of their lungs. With his arrival, the party was underway. Lisa likened the gathering to a gang of adolescent schoolboys; they had laid a long rubber sheet over the slope of the garden lawns, having placed a hose pipe running water at the top. The sheet, which served as a water slide, prompted those that had part taken in more than a few libations to strip naked and, throwing caution to the wind, they threw themselves down the slide, laughing and shouting. Lisa was accustomed to seeing the group of heavily muscled lean bodies walking around in various states of undress, many naked, so the revelries seemed commonplace to her.

Bull, having done his naked race up and down the slide, taking on all comers, had retired to his room to shower and dress, appearing half an hour later at his bedroom window with what appeared to be a large golfing umbrella. Clumsily, he opened it, and shouting 'Watch this lads,' he launched himself from the upstairs window onto the lawn below, fully expecting the umbrella to afford him a landing befitting Mary Poppins. However, the reality of the landing was far less than elegant, with Bull's 22 stones landing on top of Ray, who had been walking obliviously under the window when the larger than life presence alighted on his shoulders, causing him to crumble to the ground, sending them both rolling down the lawn into the shrubbery at the bottom. All hell broke loose as Ray retaliated at the assault on his person – luckily they had both had plenty to drink, making the scuffle that ensued more 'Keystone Cops' than 'Enter the Dragon'.

Gareth, shaking his head, looked at Lisa and said, 'That is the head of my task force, my bodyguard and my second in command.'

She smiled, laughing at the antics of the two as they thrashed about in the bushes. 'I am surprised you have managed to survive as long as you have, if that's the case!' She always managed to make him smile.

Getting up from the lounger, he called for a stop to the rustling of the bushes. 'Take it into the gym, lads,' he shouted, which stopped the proceedings dead. The revelries went on until the wee small hours for all but a few; Gareth always kept half a dozen of his men aside from the proceedings, sober and ready to work at a moment's notice. He left nothing to chance should unwelcome visitors call.

Gareth had to step up Lisa's security detail at an alarming rate to stem the tide of aggrieved factions whose businesses he had wiped out and who were looking for retribution. They had given up trying to find the man himself, as that proved futile, but they knew if they waited and watched Lisa's home that he would turn up sooner rather than later. He had purchased one of the terraced properties that faced Lisa's home in order to make it easier for his men to keep watch over her, as well as facilitating a place for them to meet and stay to get away from the hustle and bustle of the Bull Pen and to accommodate her staying with him without being too far from home, literally 100 yards away from where the angry hippo that was Bill Turner lay snoring his head off, uninterested and oblivious to where Lisa was or what she was doing, so wrapped up in himself that nothing else mattered. Lisa had been to the farm to check on the horses and spend time with a new litter of puppies that Jackie had bred. It was her favourite time, relaxing with puppies climbing all over her, catching up on Jackie's news. Having spent a couple of hours there, feeling thoroughly relaxed and refreshed, she headed home to prepare dinner for Bill and Edward, who had moved back home from his grandmother's. As Edward had grown into a teenager, he became increasingly more reactive, acting out. Lisa found him difficult to deal with, especially when the police became involved. Mixing with the wrong sort, she was told by the officer that visited her home. Gareth had intervened, not wanting Lisa to become stressed. He made it his mission to watch Edward from the sidelines. The more he watched, the more he saw himself in the lad; it bothered him to the extent that he started working out the dates. Dear God, this could be my son, he thought, his mind in a whirl. Why had Lisa not come to the same conclusion? he questioned. He resolved to get a hair

145

sample to have a paternity test done, but how to get the sample without alerting the lad to what was going on?

As Lisa left the farm that day, she was aware that Mac and Ray were part of her security detail, having told them that she was leaving the farm, Mac in the vehicle in front of Lisa and Ray in the vehicle tailing her. The distance from Lisa's home to the farm was seven miles, and halfway through the journey an Audi R4 containing four men overtook Ray at speed, drawing level with Lisa's white Combi van, trying to force it off the road. Lisa struggled to keep control, ending up on the verge, shaken to say the least. Ray caught up with the vehicle as they were about to alight and take Lisa hostage. Taking in the scene in a flash, he fired one shot straight at them, sending them running in fear for their vehicle. They sped off with Ray in hot pursuit. Mac doubled back, having had a call from Ray to escort Lisa home. Lisa was still on the verge and visibly shaken when Mac reached her, so he sat with her for a while, letting her gather her composure, while he contacted Gareth to bring him up to speed on what had happened. Gareth, on hearing the update, immediately relayed the registration number of the vehicle to his contact, who furnished him with a name and address that he recognised, causing him to head towards Manchester at speed. He knew where this lowlife was heading and the warehouse that he used for his shady dealings. Ray followed the vehicle to the outskirts of Manchester, where it pulled down a side street. Without thinking, outraged that they would dare to try and take Lisa in broad daylight, he followed down the narrow street that was lined with warehouses. As his vehicle pulled in behind them a third vehicle immediately pulled in behind Ray's, blocking his exit. The four he had chased jumped into action as Ray stood and waited for them to bring it on. He was mindful of the four who had just joined the party and were now walking down the street towards him. The four men were woefully outclassed as Ray unleashed every ounce of fury he was feeling, taking them apart in seconds. As he turned to face the second wave that were just within reach, one was no longer in sight giving him cause for concern as the three heavyweights weighed in together, trying to overpower Ray. He struggled to free himself as he felt the cold hard steel of a knife pierce his lower back at kidney level. The pain ripping through his body caused him to gasp out loud. The four seized their advantage, one on each arm, the third holding his head back, and the fourth punching Ray in the gut, causing blood to gush from the deep wound they had inflicted.

The assailant holding his head back took out a cutthroat razor, saying, 'Let's give the pretty boy a permanent smile, shall we?' They all laughed.

'No, I don't think so.' The voice echoed off the warehouse walls that lined both sides of the street. Seeing the face of the man they feared walking towards them, shadowed by Bull and Steve, they dropped Ray to the floor, his body limp and unresponsive. Gareth exploded, knocking two to the ground, Bull and Steve ripping into the remaining two, all eight now lying unconscious as Gareth retrieved the cutthroat razor he always carried in his boot.

'I am going to give these fuckers permanent smiles,' he growled. He cut with surgical precision through each face from ear to ear, making sure that each and every one of them would be reminded of what they had done every time they looked in the mirror. Turning, he saw Ray's body oozing lifeblood. Telling Bull and Steve to load him into the vehicle quickly, he took out his gun, ending the lives of two, the one who had wielded the knife stabbing Ray being the first to go. Steve was given the keys to Ray's car and told to drive it home and to burn out the vehicles that remained.

Gareth drove like the wind back to the Bull Pen, mindful that Bull was in the back trying to stem the flow of blood leaching from Ray's body. He had called the Doc to attend and stated the reason he needed him. On their arrival they were met by Chris and Rick, who carried Ray into the house. They had made up a fully equipped hospital bed in the second lounge and the doc had set up a saline drip and blood bag to replace the precious fluid that Ray was still losing at an alarming rate. Gareth had purchased all the necessary equipment needed to run a small operating theatre; it was imperative that his men received the best treatment possible without the involvement of the authorities. The doc x-rayed Ray to ascertain how deep the wound was and what damage had been done. Luckily, it had missed his kidneys by a fraction. The doc, with Bull in attendance, administered morphine, and having cleaned the area with iodine started to work, stitching the different layers of flesh involved, first tying off the major blood vessel that had been severed. When they were satisfied that the wound was closed and there was no further blood loss, they made Ray comfortable. The doc told Gareth that he had done all that he could, but there had been a dangerous amount of blood loss. It was now up to how much strength Ray had to pull him through. Gareth called Lisa and asked her to come to the Bull Pen, that she may need to say goodbye to Ray. She was there in the blink of an eye, and as she walked into the lounge where Ray laid, her heart filled with dread as she saw his face, ghostly white and bloodied from the beating he had taken. Barely conscious, he reached out to her, grabbing her hand. With what little strength he had left, he pulled her into his arms. She buried her head into his chest and wept bitter tears. He seemed to visibly relax, and drifted off into a fitful sleep with Lisa curled up beside him on his bed.

Every time she made to move, he would say 'Please stay with me,' and stay she did through the long night. As dawn broke, Gareth came into the room to see if all was as it should be, telling Lisa that the doc was due to come and check on Ray to replenish his fluids and pain management. She followed Gareth through to the main lounge to have a hot drink and gather her thoughts.

'How on earth did this happen to him? Is he going to recover?' she sobbed.

'He took down four big guys, but there were more that overpowered him. He did well, Lisa, he is a strong lad, he will pull through this,' he reassured her, although he was unsure in his heart of hearts that it would be so. The doc came daily to redress the wound and administer antibiotics, fluids, and pain relief.

When he was unable to attend, Bull took over, the consummate professional in all things when called to step up to the mark. His joker mantle cast aside, he was the one who stitched and tended wounds, proving to be an exemplary student of the Docs teachings. It took Ray a month to recover from his ordeal, Lisa spending many late-night vigils by his bedside. During one such occasion Ray declared that he had fallen deeply in love with Lisa, a fact that Lisa dismissed, believing it to be the declaration of a man on his death bed. He was up and about after the fourth week, much to Lisa and Gareth's relief. Ray had repaid his debt to Lisa, making sure that those who sought to take her were punished and a clear and present warning issued to all who may follow in their footsteps. Gareth was in no doubt that there would be many more such incidents; his empire's reach now spanned most of the United Kingdom. He was later to remind Ray of his death bed declaration and of the fact that he didn't die. Ray just smiled. He adored Lisa, and nothing would change that fact.

The early morning light streamed into the lounge as Lisa drank her breakfast brew. Sumo, her Dobermann male, lay head resting on her lap, her mind replaying her life in vivid detail. Stroking the magnificent dog's head, she spoke to him, his eyes telling her that he understood every word. 'How did I get here, my love? It's just as if I am watching a gangster film.' Lifting his head, he cocked it to one side in sympathy to his mistress' plight. She rolled his ear backwards and forwards as he closed his eyes, relaxing at her touch. She mused whether if she had stayed with Gareth all those years ago he would have taken the same path, or could she have taken him on a more peaceful journey through life? It was difficult enough fitting two lives into one, but now that Gareth demanded to see more and more of her it was only possible because Bill did not give a damn about where she was or what she was doing, too wrapped up in his own tiny world to notice what was going on under his nose. He was basically just a lodger. He had failed as a partner and as a father to Edward, showing no interest in the boy other than to antagonise him and pull him down, but as long as he brought in a wage to keep the house bills paid and the food on their plates she was willing to allow him to stay, even though Gareth was straining at the leash to get at him, the only thing barring his way being Lisa. Even after all the things that Bill had done and said to her, she could not see him subjected to what she knew Gareth had in mind for him, that was far too final for her. He did serve his purpose, in a way: he stopped Gareth from moving in and taking over her life completely. Throughout her life, men had always sought to control her by violence, verbal abuse, by degrading her, yet with Gareth it was totally different and, in many respects, harder to deal with. All that he did was for her, she was the focus of his attention at all times and in all things. Her personal safety was akin to that of the royal family; he made sure that no one could get near her. She was older and wiser now, not in the first flush of youthful passion, and her independent nature was firmly fixed in place – she had to be independent to survive her choice of partners, all of whom fell way short of being providers. At times, with Gareth, she felt suffocated by his presence, always touching, stroking, making sure that all her needs were met, that she was comfortable. He wanted her to have everything her heart desired, but he wanted her close, the closer the better. He carried with him at all times a very expensive diamond engagement ring and asked her to marry him every few weeks, only to be disappointed by her non-committal answers, yet he never gave up hope. She had rocked him to his foundation when she told him that a cage was a cage, even if the bars were gold and not steel. She would graciously accept gifts from him, but his money was his own and she would not take his money when she could not commit to him. She had been conditioned over the years to accept indifference from the men in her life, making Gareth's lavish attentions seem excessive and unnecessary to her. She was his and always would be, she adored him with every fibre of her being; he was her true soulmate, he knew her better than she knew herself, she could hide nothing from him. He knew the size and style of clothes she liked and always brought presents that fitted her to perfection, while she always got it wrong when shopping for herself. She was his grand obsession, and therein lay the problem. Gareth had obtained his hair sample from Edward during a skirmish with a youth Gareth had paid to antagonise the lad. He sat in his office, staring at the envelope, not wanting to open it, yet he needed to know. The letter opener sliced through the envelope top, revealing its contents. Taking a deep breath he removed the letter and slowly took in the information that it contained. His heart leaped in his chest. 'I am a father, he is my son!' The words he read explained that the findings were 99 percent sure. He needed to break the news to Lisa, along with another snippet of information that he would have to approach with a degree of sensitivity.

Gareth had taken on a contract many months ago and was just waiting for the right set of circumstances to present themselves. He would have to be away from Lisa and that was not something he could tolerate too often; he had made her a promise that this would be the last. He also needed to speak to her about the revelation of Edward's parentage. He had shipped his weapon of choice, a long-range state-of-the-art rifle, packed in a wooden casket lined with canisters of fish oil to mask the true contents from the x-ray machines to a forwarding address in Panama City. He would leave the country under one of any number of identities, altering his appearance to suit the passport he would be using. He told Lisa not to contact him, that he would contact her after a week and let her know he was ok. She could not bear the thought of being away from him, and the fact that he was going to South America only served to add to her anxiety. The day before his departure they shared a romantic dinner at the Bull Pen. He had ordered the lads out for the evening so that they could have peace and quiet for their time together. His love for her had grown in intensity over the years; all he focused on was pleasing her. Gareth had collected her from home, taking her to the Bull Pen to say their goodbyes before his departure. As they walked through the door, he took her in his arms. Cupping her face in his hands he looked deeply, longingly into her eyes and kissed her with every atom of passion that flowed through his veins, nipping and sucking her lips, searching her mouth. His tongue entwined with hers, she stopped for a moment.

'You have had your tongue pierced,' she giggled.

'All the better to eat you with, my dear,' he replied, and there it was, the smile that got him everything he desired. Holding her close to his body, he lifted her from the floor. She automatically wrapped her legs around his waist, feeling the hardness of his erection growing against her sex. No smart comments this time, she was lost in the moment, wondering if he would come back to her. He carried her through to the bedroom where they undressed each other slowly, savouring every moment, every reveal, kissing and caressing every inch of exposed flesh. She marvelled at the sight of his naked body, heavily muscled and cut, not an ounce of spare flesh anywhere to be seen. On reaching his manhood her eyes lit up with excitement. 'You have put a bolt through Rodger. I have heard about them heightening the sensation, you wicked man,' she grinned.

'Let us see then, shall we? It's only just been done and is tender to say the least.' His eyes brimming with lust, he pushed her down on the bed. He pulled her naked body down the bed toward him, and instinctively she threw her legs over his shoulders. He buried his head in the cleft of her legs, forcing his tongue into her swollen, juicy quim, lapping, sucking, licking her clitoris.

'Oh dear God,' she moaned, 'why didn't you have your tongue pierced before it's – Oh God Oh God!' she cried out as he took her to the edge of her orgasm. Forcing her legs open, he pushed his rock hard erection into her slick warm depths. The bolt, having caused extra swelling, heightened all sensations for both of them. Even the pain from the partially healed piercing gave him a jolt of ecstasy that he had never experienced before, giving a whole new meaning to pleasure and the pain as the two mingled to push them both over the edge. They made love like it was their last day on earth; nothing and no one else mattered as they became one.

Gareth had made alterations to the Bull Pen over the years, building a state-of-the-art stables and indoor arena, having brought in two magnificent sports horses to fill the void left by Jake. Riding always bought him closer to Lisa, even when she was not in his life. Jasper, a magnificent 17.2 hand tall Grey, and Jake II, a 16.3 hands bright Bay were schooled to perfection before he purchased them, paying a king's ransom for them both. He had also developed an obsession with muscle cars, having a building that was originally meant to be stables now fully heated and housing a collection that was worth many millions of pounds. They walked around the property, visiting the magnificent equines, and finally ending up at his collection of cars. Her eyes always lit up with delight when he revealed his latest acquisition. He removed the black custom made covers from each in their turn to reveal a Maclaren Mercedes, Maserati C12 Sports, Koenigsegg Agera, Bugatti Veyron, Porsche Carrera, his first love in cars, and his current chariot of fire, the Lamborghini Murciélago, which bore the number plates Lisa 1.

'This is your car, my sweet, as is everything that I own if anything should happen to me.' The tone of his voice was serious, reverting to the legal eagle speak that he used at his practice. 'You would become a very wealthy woman in your own right.' Had he been declaring this revelation to any other woman they would have been elated, yet it served only to fill Lisa with nothing but foreboding. Why would he make this declaration now? Was he not expecting to return from his trip abroad? The worst case scenarios played over and over in her mind. He could see that she was struggling with his words. 'It is merely a way of my always taking care of you, it has been in place for quite some time now. I made my will many years ago when you first left me.' The thought of that day brought a lump to his throat.

Always acutely aware of his emotional discomfort, she reached for his hand and squeezed it tenderly. 'Your money means nothing to me, it is you that I care about and always have.' His eyes welled like limpid pools of crystal blue. She always knew exactly what to say to ease whatever troubled his mind.

'I have bought you a pair of Christian Louboutin leopard print shoes babe, will you wear them for me with nothing else and stretch yourself out over the bonnet of the Murciélago so that I can have a photograph of you for my wallet?' he pleaded, with that world class smile that unlocked any inhibitions she may have had.

'Cheeky, but how could I refuse that request?' The glint in her eyes said it all. He produced the shoes magically, having secreted them near the cars. She undressed slowly, tantalisingly, while he watched her every move hungrily. She placed the exotic shoes on her feet, struggling to get her balance in the four-inch heels. 'I am going to get a nosebleed up here, and broken ankles,' she giggled, making him double over with laughter.

He had set up a camera on a tripod. Helping her up onto the bonnet of the Lambo, he stood to one side as she posed, his eyes filled with lust. In seconds he was undressed, and before she could make a smart remark, he had spun her round, her legs around his waist, her rump on the bonnet. He rammed his aching erection deep inside her, making her cry out. He powered into her warm depths, the one place he found release and comfort, until they both exploded in unison. They walked through the gardens, laughing and chatting in the afterglow of their love, whole, complete, at ease, as if as one.

'I have something that I need to tell you, sweetheart,' he proffered, looking deeply into her eyes.

'What is it?' she queried.

'There is no easy way to bring this to your attention other than just to say it,' he faltered.

'Get on with it, then.'

Her impatience made him smile, as he knew that what he had to say would shock her to her core. 'Edward is my son, sweetheart.'

He watched her face as her smart mouth kicked in. 'Don't be stupid, how could he be—' stopping mid-way through her comeback, her brain had done the math, and the look on her face was priceless as the realisation hit home. 'How do you know that?' she queried.

'I had a paternity test done. I managed to get a sample and the findings were conclusive.' The questions came thick and fast until the reality of the situation became clear to her. 'I haven't done anything about it yet, I want to give you time to come to terms with it and discuss a course of action with you, but that will have to wait until after my trip.' She nodded in agreement, still stunned at the news. It was time for her to return home, his parting words gave her little comfort. 'This is a routine trip, nothing has been left to chance. It has been planned a long time now and I will be back before you know it. Just don't contact me, I will ring you when it's done and I am on my way home.' He kissed her deeply before she climbed out of the car.

He had everything prepared at the Bull Pen, all he needed to do was to fit the wig, prosthetic mask, and dentures that altered his appearance, a skill he had learned from the makeup artists that made up the different masks and profiles to suit each of the many passports that he possessed. Looking in the mirror, he smiled at the stranger that looked back at him, satisfied that even the sharpest airport official could not detect any imperfections in his new identity. Walking to his closet, he unzipped a suit guard to reveal numerous sets of ghost plates for each of the many vehicles that he and the lads owned. Taking one that matched his Range Rover Sports, he fitted them, loading a leather sports bag into the car. He had briefed Bull, Ray and Steve on matters that needed their attention and told them no contact; there was also a plan of action in place should he fail to return. Even then, Lisa's safety was paramount: her security detail was in place and stepped up in his absence. This trip would add three million to swell the coffers, his services always commanding the ultimate tariff as he never failed to accomplish the tasks he was contracted to carry out. The animal that he was going to terminate had killed a 35-year-old pregnant woman and her two children, aged three and five, in a case of mistaken identity. Her wealthy father had commissioned Gareth's services, knowing that he would not fail him in his time of grief.

Lisa could not eat or sleep, her mind working overtime, longing for his return. The lads kept her occupied, calling in for a quick chat and a brew, helping to keep her spirits high. On the evening of the fifth day, Lisa's phone rang. Her heart leapt into her throat seeing Gareth's number flash onto the screen. As she answered, she heard his deep, rich, cultured tones.

'I am at Heathrow, be with you soon sweetheart. I have missed you so much, all went to plan, I am ok.'

'I was so worried,' she said, her voice breaking as she sobbed in relief. He was gone in an instant, heading home to be at her side; he would not leave her again. Gareth had checked his offshore account to satisfy himself that his fee had been paid in full, and he was not disappointed. He had gifted a second hit at the same time, recognising a cartel assassin in his sights. One less lowlife to infest the world. Gareth had just showered and changed as Bull arrived with Lisa; he had unpacked his rifle, a Sako TRG-42, considered to be the best in its class, having been delivered home that day. In the main lounge at the Bull Pen was a storage place under the floor; it had been deepened, widened and lead-lined, undetectable when the wooden door was dropped and a rug pulled over it. This was where Gareth keep his valuables: a considerable amount of gold and gems, plus some of his higher calibre weaponry. Lisa jumped into his arms before he managed to place the weapon back in its allotted space for safe keeping. She wrapped her legs round his waist and sobbed with relief as his strong arms enfolded her, burying her head in his neck. He felt her tears like raindrops on his bare flesh.

'I am here, sweetheart, and I will never leave you again, I swear this to you.' His voice trembled with emotion as he held her close, feeling the tension leave her body. He had thought long and hard about all the time that he had lost not knowing that Edward was his and how different things could have been for the boy had he had his guidance instead of the indifference that Bill Turner had shown him. He did not know how to broach the subject with the lad, knowing full well that he would reject the facts and come out fighting. Lisa was of the same mind, that it would be best left until the right moment presented itself.

Their tantric lessons had become a regular feature at the Bull Pen, with increasing interest from the lads, who had been granted limited access to the proceedings to see if they would be interested in developing their own skills in that direction, although none had significant others in their lives; it proved to be far too intimate for the super fit single males, many excusing themselves. Only Mac was intrigued with the teachings, as his sex life had been sadly lacking and loveless, only knowing his wife, from whom he was now divorced. Paul and Liz had a progressive open relationship that allowed them to see other people to practice the tantric teachings. Their relationship happily spanned many years without any problems; however, that had begun to change as her fascination with Gareth began to grow. He always entered the class with jogging bottoms on, painfully aware that one pair of eyes was watching his every move. Liz could not take her eyes off him; the easy graceful way that he moved, likened to a big cat on the prowl, a legacy of his Shaolin teachings, always in perfect balance, and a body that was ripped and toned to perfection proved to mesmerise. She wanted to touch to experience the feel of his body, but had been warned that he could not tolerate any other woman than Lisa and that he would react very badly should his personal space be invaded. Nonsense, she thought, how could he resist me? Lisa is nothing by comparison. Unbeknownst to anyone, she had secreted a camera away in order to take photographs of him without anyone's knowledge. Had he known what she was doing he would have thrown her off the property, as no one was allowed to photograph him, even reporters covering some of the high-profile cases he worked on were forbidden under pain of prosecution to take images of him. The first time that her covert actions came to light was when Paul arrived home to find a full-size portrait of Gareth framed and hung in their lounge. He had a feeling as if she had cheated on their relationship, having a photograph of one of their clients on the wall of their home, and secondly one of foreboding; this could cause problems with Gareth, as they were in a position of trust, a trust that Liz had broken and flaunted.

Paul confronted her about the image on the wall and asked if there were any more, to which she replied, 'No. What harm is there in my having a photograph of him?' she questioned.

'He is a prominent legal professional and businessman, for one, and secondly, you have broken his trust in us as professional teachers who have access to his home.' His tone was one that she was not used to hearing; he was usually a placid, peace-loving man, but this obviously had upset him deeply. Paul was not a jealous man by nature, having had a strong open relationship with Liz for many years, but at the back of his mind there was something that bothered him greatly about this. His trust in his partner was shaken to its core. He resolved to tell Gareth of what he had found and leave the outcome up to him. On hearing the news Gareth exploded and insisted that all copies and negatives be given to him, and that Liz no longer accompanied Paul during the lessons; she was no longer welcome at the Bull Pen. That was far less than Paul expected, and it was agreed that he undertook their lessons alone. Liz could not believe that she was no longer allowed access to the Bull Pen and resolved to challenge Gareth and ask him to recant his decision. Turning up at the Bull Pen unannounced was a definite taboo and would only serve to outrage Gareth even further. Luckily, Bull managed to intercept Liz and convinced her that Gareth was away on business, whilst imparting his worldly wisdom on the etiquette required regarding visiting the property. When Paul received the phone call from Gareth, he was both apologetic and outraged at Liz's cavalier attitude. Gareth informed him that an injunction would be put in force should Liz attempt to trespass on his property again. Once the call was finished, Paul went to their room and started to look through their things. He no longer trusted Liz, and sure enough, in her underwear drawer, under the drawer lining paper, he found several more photographs of Gareth. His mind in turmoil, he rang Liz and told her of his findings and that he wanted her gone from his life, he felt betrayed by her and didn't want her near him, and to collect her things and leave as soon as possible. The incidence served to end their longstanding relationship and business venture, which meant that Paul needed to find another Tantric Master to teach his classes alongside him.

Lisa railed against the constant intrusion into her daily life, Gareth assigning a man to help her around the home, as living with Bill Turner's slovenly habits caused her endless stress, and a further four men outside, two per vehicle, one driving the locale, checking for suspect vehicles, the other parked covertly, watching all comings and goings. 'It's like living in a goldfish bowl,' she complained to Gareth. He imparted against his better judgement that the wife of one of his men had been shot whilst in bed and that he needed to make sure that nothing of that nature ever happened to her. He always shielded her from that sort of information, knowing that she would drop into panic mode; after all, he had painted a target on her back, as she often reminded him. He always shielded her from the reality of his work, protecting her emotional as well as physical well being. She had noticed that someone seemed to have been in her home whilst she had been out and exploded when she discovered that Gareth and his men had keys to her home to enable them to check that all was clear for her return from trips away to the farm or shops, her dogs being accustomed to their new friends' comings and goings. All this activity going on under Turner's nose, to which he was oblivious. As he walked in from work, they would walk out of the back door, vaulting the garden fence into the school grounds. Gareth was acutely aware of Lisa's stress levels reaching meltdown, and to that end he instructed the lads that were available to call into see her to brighten her day, not that they needed any instruction, as all were drawn to her, as always, like moths to the flame. She was their Queen Bee, the highlight of their day was her visits to the Bull Pen. She only had to walk in and sit down: Gareth would bring her a huge cushion adorned with a Dobermann head plus an expensive throw that matched to cover her should she need it, and once she alighted they would appear as if drawn by magnets, unable to resist her lilting laughter and smart-mouthed quips. They revelled in the way she attacked Gareth, she was the only being walking this earth that was allowed to get away with it; he was a puppy dog around her, a side of him they had never seen before. He behaved as if there was only the two of them there, finding the pummelling that she gave him a turn on, the result of which being apparent to all present – at that point he would pick her up, throwing her over his shoulder and walking through to their bedroom. It always served to embarrass Lisa, causing to bury her head in his neck, as they all knew what was coming next.

Eileen had been a close personal friend of Ann Edwards for many years, meeting up for outings on a weekly basis, always in touch by phone. It had been over a week now since Eileen had managed to reach Ann by phone, and longer still since one of their weekly luncheons. Bearing that in mind, she decided to make an impromptu visit to Ann's home, running the risk of annoying Ann, who frowned on unscheduled visitors to her property. On reaching Ann's home, she found the security gate open, and Ann's Aston Martin Vantage parked outside the main entrance. After ringing the doorbell for some ten minutes, Eileen tried the door, finding it locked. She was beginning to feel uneasy as she started to hammer at the heavily ornate wooden door. Walking to the rear of the property, she tried the kitchen door. Again, it was locked. She could see a pool of liquid on the work surface from a china cup that lay on its side, having been tipped over, the fluid dripping onto the floor. That was so out of character, she thought, Ann, who was all about image and style. Returning to her car, Eileen rang round several of Ann's acquaintances, enquiring if they had seen her. After seven calls, getting the no show from them all, she rang the local emergency services, asking for police, fire, and ambulance to attend as she feared the worst. The police were the first on the scene, but their attempts to break down the front door failed. It took the fire brigade to prise the door lock with a spreader that they used on mangled cars involved in accidents. As the door gave way, the sickening gut-wrenching smell that permeated the air bore witness to what they were about to discover. The ambulance arrived, the paramedics knowing instantly that their services would not be needed as they entered the lounge. Ann's body lay behind the lounge door, and it was believed that she had been dead two, maybe three days. There were no signs of injury and the paramedics seemed certain that a heart attack was the cause of death, although that would be left up to the local coroner's officer to ascertain, the incident now being treated as a sudden death. It was with a heavy heart that Eileen rang Gareth to inform him of his mother's death. She was certainly not expecting the reaction that greeted her.

Gareth answered the house phone at the Bull Pen, listening intently to what was being said. As Eileen finished giving her heartfelt condolences, his reply came from the depths of the coldest place in hell where he had stored it away, festering: 'I am glad she is gone, I hope she rots in hell.'

'That is your mother, Gareth, why would you say such a terrible thing?' He took pains to tell her exactly why he felt as he did, although he left out the sexual abuse, not being able to stomach saying it out loud to anyone other than Lisa. She was rocked to her core by the fact that the woman she knew as her closest and dearest friend she did not know at all. She felt betrayed, she would have helped the beautiful little blond-haired boy had she known. She had looked after him for weeks when they went away on extended holidays together. She mulled over what she had heard over the phone and headed towards the Bull Pen to better understand what she had been told. Gareth was surprised to see her, but took great pains to explain what he had endured from the age of four from both the people that passed themselves off as his parents, leaving out the deviant behaviour of his mother. Eileen was absolutely gutted that she was unaware of the cruelty that was going on, perpetrated by a woman that she called friend. As Eileen left, she informed Gareth of the details of the funeral arrangements and that there would be a large attendance once the coroner had released her body. Gareth had made up his mind that he would attend the service, with Lisa at his side. On the day of the funeral, the church that had been the venue for his grandparents' funerals was packed with acquaintances from polite society circles, all offering their condolences at the sudden and tragic passing of one of their number. Gareth stood with Lisa, listening to the steady stream of eulogies singing the praises of the morally bankrupt bitch who caused him nothing but pain. Gareth had refused the opportunity of giving a eulogy, not being able to trust himself to remain under control.

As he led the long line of people ready to file past the coffin, holding tightly on to Lisa's hand for comfort and reassurance, he drew level with the expensively ornate coffin and, turning to face it, he thumped the lid heavily with his clenched fist and declared at the top of his voice for the whole congregation to hear, 'Rot in hell, you evil bitch, for ruining my life.' The gasp from those in attendance was followed by a deathly silence. They were all now aware that something was very much amiss for an only son to react in that manner at the funeral of his mother.

Many of the men present patted his back, not daring to ask questions, although they gravitated to Eileen, who was heard to say, 'It appears that all was not as it seemed.' Lisa, hearing her explanation, thought that she deserved to know the full extent of her best friend's depravity. Taking her aside, she watched as the woman's reaction turned to one of disgust and loathing as Lisa recounted the catalogue of sickening abuse that Gareth had suffered at the hands of the woman she called friend. She wrapped her arms around Gareth and sobbed, apologising for not seeing what was going on. He patted her shoulder and assured her that a weight had been lifted from his world now that his mother was dead and not to trouble herself about it further.

It had been many years since Gareth's skirmish with the Russians, and he was surprised to receive a call from a Russian contact requesting an unsanctioned rematch to be held at a venue of his choosing. The Russians did not do defeat easily and were pushing to take down the man that was one of the highest-ranking undefeated kickboxers of his age. They mistakenly thought that his advancing years would have diminished his skills. The venue chosen by Gareth was his club in Manchester, as it had a huge cellar area that had been decorated to accommodate large functions without bothering the rich and famous that frequented its lavishly appointed premises upstairs. The ring was set up, as well as seating for 300-400 punters, all eager to lay wagers as to the outcome of the grudge match. Only those who had known Gareth a while were aware that he was a skilled martial artist, most fully expecting to see the wealthy entrepreneur bite the dust in a blood fest. The bets that were laid seemed to lean towards the Russian having a resounding win; that is, until Gareth's own men started to bet on the outcome, laying down hundreds of thousands of pounds in his favour. They had no doubt of the outcome at all. Extra security was called for, in case of trouble, and Gareth's army surrounded outside as well as inside, a formidable squad, all dressed to intimidate. Gareth had agreed to the rematch only on the understanding that, no matter what the outcome, this would be the end of the matter. As the room filled, the atmosphere was electric with anticipation. All those in attendance had been searched for arms of any description, which they were obliged to leave with security until they vacated the club. Lisa was dressed to impress in a designer gown, a present from Gareth. She looked radiant, he thought, as he kissed her deeply. He watched as she walked towards the ladies' rest room he could not take his eyes away from the glorious vision before him. He noticed a group of four women leave their seats and follow Lisa into the rest room. They had been unable to take their eyes of him and were miffed that he had ignored them for the woman they felt was lesser than them. They were the type he found abhorrent, heavily made up with artificially plumped lips and silicone breasts, clothes that were spray painted on, leaving little to the imagination; the type that always tried to catch his eye and took offence when he ignored their advances. They looked down on Lisa; how on earth could he be with her when he could have any one of them? How dare he ignore them. As Lisa entered the rest room the four women followed her through the doors.

Their leader, a leggy blonde Barbie clone in her early forties, waited for Lisa to leave the cubicle to wash her hands. 'Well, well, what have we here then? I think someone is way out of her depth, don't you girls?' They all grinned, nodding in a menacing fashion. 'What on God's earth does he see in you I wonder?'

Lisa finished drying her hands and turned to face the group, who had formed a semi-circle behind her. 'Are you speaking to me?' she asked.

'Oh, a local yokel by the sounds of that accent. Yes, you are the only peasant in here. Why don't you collect your coat and leave? You are out of your class, dear.' Lisa felt threatened, although more than equal to the task; she would not be put down by these grotesque caricatures.

As their leader took a step towards her the door burst open and Gareth walked in. 'Lisa, are you ok sweetheart?' he enquired.

'I think you are in the wrong restroom, handsome, can I help you?'

'No you cannot, you dirty whore.' He spat the words in her face.

'How dare you speak to me in that manner?' Her tone was shocked; no man had ever disrespected her in that way.

Gareth had heard the whole conversation from outside the door and was furious. 'Get your belongings and get out of the club,' he barked at them.

'You have no right to order us of the premises,' she argued.

'Oh, I assure you, I have the only right; the club is mine, and as of now every one of you is barred.' Her jaw dropped has he took out his phone and spoke to his security, asking them to come to the ladies' rest room to remove four whores that were to be barred admission to the club in future. As security man handled the four hags to the door, Gareth wrapped his arms around Lisa to comfort her.

'I had it under control, you know,' she chirped, making him laugh uncontrollably.

'I don't doubt that for one minute. I think you should be the one climbing into the ring, not me.' Taking her hand, he led her to the ringside, seeing her settled in her front row seat.

The Russian was a great deal younger than Gareth in years, but not appearance. His body large/ heavily muscled and ripped, he sat in his corner, a brooding presence watching intently as Gareth stepped into the ring. Walking to his corner he removed his gi top to reveal the Dragon tattoo of the club that trained him, many of its members being present to watch their sensei in action. The ladies present marvelled at the sight of his ripped, toned torso, belying his years; he appeared as if 35 years old to them. The scene set, all bets placed and safely in the hands of security, the gladiators called into the ring centre by the referee, the match began. Gareth was acutely aware that this youngster had power but poor technique, knowing full well that he could finish him in seconds, but he needed to put on a show for those who had paid heavily to see a fight. He played with the Russian like a big cat taunting its prey until he grew bored. Seeing his opening, he landed one blow that sent the Russian crashing to the canvas, out for the count. It was under a minute and the crowd erupted, feeling cheated at the outcome being over and done with so easily when they had come wanting blood. Security quickly stepped up to the mark, quelling outbreaks of dissention amongst the glitterati in attendance, many whom had lost considerable amounts of money betting against the victor. Gareth's men made a killing that night, pushing their bank accounts into the millions in some cases, their faith in their boss and his abilities paying dividends. The Russians were far from happy but had to concede that the fight was fairly and squarely won. During the proceedings one of their number had seen and recognised Mac as being a cage fighter that they had seen in action some years ago and, approaching Gareth, they enquired as to his status and said that they had a contender training in the United States that had been trying to track him down, knowing that he was undefeated and the one opponent to beat. Mac was consulted and it was agreed that a no rules cage bout would be scheduled at the same venue, at a time to be arranged. Gareth put Mac into training immediately, bumping up his protein intake with fillet steaks twice daily. His daily workout routine only needed a little fine tuning to meet the criteria required to boost his stamina for the no holds barred match with the America-based Ukrainian. Mac was known for the ferocity of his blows, none of his opponents being able to stand against his onslaughts; every inch of his formidably ripped muscle mass went into delivering each bone-crunching blow, leaving his opponents crushed, disabled, unable to go on.

Gareth had been true to his word when it came to finding Mac's family and reuniting them, making it easy for them to join Mac's life in a guarded, safe way, them being oblivious to the darker side of his life. However, his brother, who had been wrongly imprisoned for six years, serving 18 months before Gareth proved beyond a shadow of a doubt through the use of CCTV footage that he was innocent and secured him close to a million in compensation, was exactly the stamp of individual that Gareth required. Stuart had the typical Bolshevik attitude driven by his need for the adrenaline fix that was ever present and necessary during his time in prison, keeping him alive, making the other inmates wary. Gareth could see much of his younger self in Stuart, but was under no illusions that his would not be an easy transition into his organisation. Mac's older brother had also served a prison sentence, during which time he had learned a trade, becoming a chef. Gareth took Ian into his home, where he became housekeeper and chef. He carried the same name as Mac, both being called Ian by the hospitals that looked after them when they were abandoned. The third of the four Macdonald brothers was Anthony, a quiet man, the youngest of the four at 44 years of age. Anthony was a handy lad to have about, as with his brothers he was well able to handle himself in a fight, being able to turn his hand to any manner of task, joinery being his forte. The Macdonald brothers and their sister were the result of a union between two drug addicts, their mother giving every one of their children up at birth and, in Mac's case, leaving him on the hospital steps, umbilical cord still wet. Gareth's interest in his own background was piqued when Eileen mentioned during one of her visits that his mother had gone through a second pregnancy, the resulting child being given up for adoption on the instructions of Brian Edwards. Gareth set in motion the team of private investigators that he always used for his legal work. He was not prepared for what they discovered, the facts of which shocked him to his foundation. It seemed that Ann Edwards had returned to her handsome farmer a second time, resulting in a younger full brother to Gareth, plus a half-brother, the result of the farmer's own marriage. Not only that, but Ann had a third pregnancy to a young man that she had a dalliance with, handing the boy child back to him for him to rear on his own. Gareth had gone from being alone to having three brothers in the blink of an eye. David was the first of the brothers to introduce himself to Gareth, accepting his invitation to lunch at the Bull Pen. He needed Lisa at his side for moral support, plus she always enchanted male visitors helping them to relax. An accountant by trade, a confident 45-year-old standing at six foot one with a toned, lean body, brilliant blue eyes and spiky blonde hair, there was no doubting the that they were brothers. They greeted each other with a hearty hug and back patting, typical of most male family members. During their lunch David told Gareth that when his father was on his deathbed Ann Edwards had visited him and told him of the existence of Gareth. He could see no earthly reason for making him aware at that time other than to perhaps obtain money from him. Before his father's death he had instructed David to find Gareth and help him, should he need it. David quickly realised that Gareth was far from needing his help and, in fact, before the end of their first meeting Gareth had secured his services for his entire organisation. He was thoroughly mesmerised by Lisa, thinking his brother a very lucky man for being with such a pleasant lady, who was a breath of fresh air. Some weeks later David moved into the Bull Pen, wanting to be closer to the brother he had just found. The second of the brothers to accept a luncheon appointment at the Bull Pen was Edward, known as Ed, a fireman. At 54 years of age he was almost a clone of his elder brother Gareth, so much so that he took Lisa's breath away, the likeness was so striking.

'My God, you could be twins,' she blurted out as he was introduced. He too fell under her spell immediately, considering his newfound brother a fortunate man to have such a gem of a lady on his arm. The third brother lived in as small flat over a shop, as he had fallen on hard times when his father had died. His name was also David. Gareth, Lisa and Mac arrived at the address furnished by the detectives, a shabby rented property above a hairdresser's. David had no idea why they wanted to speak to him and was at first reluctant to let them in, thinking they were agents of his landlord as he was behind with the rent. He was as tall as his brothers and obviously had their broad frames, yet appeared thin, drawn, with dark circles round his eyes. As Gareth and Lisa spoke to him, Mac looked round trying to find the makings of a brew without much luck, as the cupboards were empty. The shock on David's face as Gareth unfolded the story of their connection worried Lisa, thinking he was so frail he couldn't stand the stress. She was right; he broke down and sobbed.

'You're coming with me, David, get your stuff together.' Gareth was adamant that he was not having him stay in that place any longer. David explained that he had very little to take with him. 'That is ok, we will get you everything that you need,' Gareth said, his heart aching for his brother and the diminished state he had found him in. Gareth had been left over 100,000 pounds in cash and two properties by his mother, but he wanted nothing to do with any of it and had decided to give the largest of the properties to David for his home base, and the money he would split between David and Ed. They were loath to accept Gareth's generosity until he explained about their mother and what she had done to him and how she owed them, assuring them that they were lucky to have escaped her attentions. They were all sickened and disgusted that she could do that to her own child;

the images in their heads served to kill any romantic notion that they may have had about the mother they never knew. They were drawn to their newfound brother and his band of merry men finding him charismatic, generous, and loyal.

Sex between Lisa and Gareth had always been the most natural joyous affair and a topic of many a conversation, Gareth always seeking to find new ways to please her to keep their love fresh and exciting. Lisa and Jackie had recently visited the cinema to see the film version of the three books that Jackie had just finished reading. Lisa mentioned the red room featured in the film and books to Gareth and it piqued his interest. Buying a copy of the book, he took in every detail of what it contained. He approached a company that specialised in custom built bedrooms of that nature, and they came and measured the room that was adjacent to their bedroom, reinforcing the walls for the frames that would hang from the ceiling, one of the work men commenting that Gareth had one lucky lady. He quickly left the man in no doubt that it was he who was the lucky one. The whole room was completed in two weeks. The lads were becoming increasingly more interested in the comings and goings but had been warned to keep away from the workmen and not to go near their bedroom. They knew by the look in his eye that this instruction was not to be ignored, under pain of serious punishment. There were ornately carved wooden chests and draws filled with all manner of sex toys: dildos of every size and shape; vibrators; rampant rabbits; nipple clamps; rows of racks with whips of every size; crops; cat o'nine tails; and beautifully crafted leather studded collars of the softest Italian leather with matching harnesses and cuffs. It was indeed kitted out in the finest way possible, a veritable palace of pleasure and pain; winches and racks with hoists; a sumptuous double bed dressed in the finest silks and satins in a rich purple colour; the walls contrasting in black and cream; the piece de resistance being a custom-built deep tan leather table that could be manipulated into any positions required, fitted with stirrups and cuffs; full length mirrors strategically placed on walls and ceiling.

Lisa was both shocked and aroused when he first showed her the room he had created just for her: shocked at the vast amount of money that he had invested in his creation, and aroused by the possibilities of using the many and varied toys that it contained. He beamed from ear to ear as he explained the uses for the instruments that the drawers contained, Lisa's eyes widening with each explanation. To say that they were both turned on was an understatement. Neither being able to resist any longer, they stripped naked Gareth lifting her and placing her on the leather table, gently placing each ankle in the stirrups and fastening anklets to hold her legs firmly in place. Next, he cuffed both her wrists, making sure that she was comfortable. He manipulated the bed's many switches until her legs were as wide apart as they could possibly go. Her arms fully outstretched, he moved them up above her head, lifting her breasts upwards, and removed the suede cat o'nine tails from its rack, the tiny glass beads knotted at the end of each strand glistening in the ambient lighting. Turning, he licked his lips; the look in his eyes alone made Lisa's nipples swell and rise, her clitoris pulse in anticipation. He circled the table, taking in every inch, growling with animalistic lust under his breath. He flicked the cat, connecting with her nipples individually, making her gasp, her sex weeping tears of desire, aching to feel the bite of the cat. Who was he to deny her every wish? He flicked the cat over her sex again and again, relishing her moans until he could bear it no longer; he needed to taste her, to feel her clitoris pulse under the caress of his tongue.

Sitting on the matching stool provided with the table, he sat between her legs, knowing that she would have to stand the intensity of his caress being unable to move. His tongue set to work. God, how he loved the sweet taste of her desire. Taking her to the edge of her release. he rose and removed the rampant rabbit from one of the many drawers, and pushing his finger into her pulsing heat he sought out her g-spot, applying rhythmic pressure. He took her yet again to the edge of her orgasm, only to withdraw. Her whole body was on fire, trembling beads of sweat covering her torso. She heard the hum of the rabbit as he switched it on, her eyes widening as it climbed to its highest setting. Looking down, she could she the glint in his eye and the wicked smile on his delectable mouth.

'For God's sake, get on with it,' she growled, panting with the exertion of struggling against the bonds that held her firmly in place, the intensity of her body having to absorb the sensation that wracked her core with the strength of ten orgasms at once. He laughed at her smart-mouthed reply. Oh, she was going to pay for that, he thought as he plunged the Rabbit deep into her moist, warm cleft. The pulse from the divine instrument against her clitoris made her whole body spasm as the full length filled her, whirling over her g-spot. She cried out, unable to move as her orgasm engulfed her as never before. That was his cue; he quickly manipulated the table, tilting it forward and bringing her sex to the right height, and rammed his steel-hard member into her depths, pounding her sex until she screamed his name and begged him to stop. Oblivious to her plea, he powered on to his release. He had never felt such force of release as now.

Unshackling Lisa, he helped her down from the table, having to support her as her legs had turned to jelly. He lifted her and placed her gently on the silk sheets of the bed before climbing in behind her as they drifted in the afterglow. They were both in full agreement that the room was definitely worth every penny spent and would bring added spice to their already extensive sexual repertoire. Lisa had never had sex with another man that made her body come alive as it did with Gareth. It was as if he was tuned into her every need and desire instinctively, knowing how to respond to her body's reactions. She was the glove that fit his hand, the object of all his desire. He wanted to possess her completely; if it had been humanly possible to crawl inside her skin and stay there, he would have made it so. He needed to be close to her constantly, touching her, stroking her, running his hands up her thigh; even when in company, engaging in conversation, he would allow his hands to run freely over her body, much to the Lisa's chagrin, as she watched their companions roll their eyes at the boldness of his actions whilst in company. Lisa found his constant attention grating at times his need to be the focus of her attention making it hard for her to relax and watch a film or TV together; his face always appeared in front of the screen, smiling the smile that got him all that he desired, his need to engage in foreplay paramount. She found him extremely needy in comparison to the other emotionally devoid partners that she had been accustomed to.

Just to test how far he would gom she asked, 'How many times could you, physically, manage to have intercourse in a 24-hour period?'

He beamed. 'Try me,' he said.

The following Sunday it was game on at the cottage. They thought that would be the safest place to avoid interruption. Their first encounter lasted two hours, after which refreshments were needed; after a 20-minute break he was locked and loaded for the second round, lasting one and a half hours. The only other break they took was for a light lunch, lasting half an hour. Eight times that day he engaged in full coitus; they spent a total of 18 hours in full on exhausting raunchy sex.

A lesson well learned, she would definitely never ask that question again, she thought, as her legs turned to jelly. For the next few days, she found sitting to be a shade problematic due to the tenderness caused by friction burns. She had never imagined that a man, no matter how fit, could keep coming back for more, especially the following day, when his appetite had returned with vengeance, to which she told him, 'Sex 'n' Travel,' her smart mouth bending him double with side-splitting laughter.

He grabbed her and kissed her deeply. 'You are my world, my reason for being, without you I am nothing. If anything happened to take you from this world, I would end my life to be with you.' His voice was filled with passion and determination, the stark truth of what he was saying rocking Lisa to her core.

'What a waste of a beautiful man that would be,' she scolded, frowning her displeasure.

The inner struggle that she battled daily was one of her fiercely independent nature against her deep love of her soulmate, a love that permeated her bones, ran through her veins and filled her core, and still she asked herself, 'Why me?' He was The Body, beautiful, powerful, rich, strong, the ultimate bad boy; every woman's dream come true, and he was hers and only hers. The long-legged slender beauties, made up to impress, that paraded before him as he visited his clubs trying to catch his attention held no sway with him; he didn't even register their presence. Those bold enough to take further steps, not accepting his indifference, usually ended up in the local A&E department.

On one such occasion, as he left his premier club, crossing to his parking space, he could see a tall, slender, heavily made up female with artificially plumped lips and breasts sat crossed legged on the bonnet of his Lamborghini Murciélago. This was the sort or woman that evoked shades of his mother, never taking no for an answer, turning his stomach.

'Get off my fucking car, you whore,' he bellowed. Profanity always sounded twice as cruel when spoken in a cultured tone.

She giggled, not taking in the enormity of her actions. 'Give me a kiss and I will oblige,' she pouted, sliding down the bonnet of the car that bore Lisa's name on its number plates.

'I will give you a kiss,' he grimaced, as he saw the scratch her heels had left behind.

The men that accompanied him froze at his answer, for they knew full well what was coming. She walked towards him, placing her hands on his chest. She didn't remember what happened next when she came round in hospital, her jaw wired shut, having been shattered by the single blow from the head that hit her full in the face. To add insult to injury, she later received a bill for five thousand pounds for the repair to the car bonnet. CCTV footage of her criminal damage to the vehicle was sent to the police; conveniently, no footage of the assault on her person was available, due to the camera having malfunctioned.

Gareth always shielded Lisa from the darker side of his dealings, yet occasionally she would be talking to one of his lads when, usually noted for being tight lipped, they would let it slip. When she heard of the incident involving his car being scratched, she wondered why he had never lost his cool with her, she had certainly given him cause over the years. He had never raised his voice in anger or lifted a hand against her during the entirety of their relationship. When she questioned him as to why, he answered, 'I could never harm or upset you in word, thought, deed or by omission. You are my world, my strength, I was put on this earth to take care of you, and I always will.' Lisa was overcome by his reply, yet would have given the world for a good old fashioned sit down and slog it out argument, which he proved incapable of, always placating her with his smile and the words, 'God, I love you to the moon and back.' How could she become angry at that? He didn't play fair at all, she thought.

Although Lisa's relationship with Bill Turner had long been over, his presence under her roof as a lodger served to stem the tide that was Gareth Edwards from rolling in and taking over. While she loved him with a passion and there would never be another for her, she found his obsessive attention suffocating, almost debilitating at times. When he was away from her, she longed to see his handsome face and hear his rich, plummy, cultured tones. When he walked through the door, she had butterflies, always melting into his arms. Their lovemaking was beyond exquisite, their sex being raunchy rough and relentless; she would never find another man who worshipped her as he did, and it frightened the hell out of her. After the initial elation of his presence, she found herself wishing him away. The more she gave of herself, the more he wanted – could she ever commit fully to him and take that walk down the aisle that he so desperately wanted? All he had to do was to ease up a little, to open his hand and let her breathe, yet that one thing seemed to be beyond his capabilities. She wanted to run at times, to be free of all the attention that he lavished on her, yet she needed his strength, his protection and his love. She wanted so much to be with him, to put an end to the dual lives that she was leading, to get rid of Bill Turner once and for all and to commit to her true love, yet she wanted to be free to do as she pleased for once in her life without having to think of others and putting their needs before her own. In her sixties now, she needed to have a phase in her life when she wasn't at the beck and call of any man. She would be with Gareth in a heartbeat if only he would lighten up. The occupants of the Bull Pen were only too aware of how she felt, as they witnessed firsthand his over-the-top attentions on a daily basis. Although they sympathised, few amongst them cared to comment. Those that did served to annoy their boss, and that was a dangerous pastime. She resolved to sit him down and discuss the problem that she had, to try and rectify the matter in a calm sensible manner. When the time came, she had her doubts, as he was in a horny mood and beaming his come-hither smile, which usually only lead to one thing.

'You can stop that right now, this is a serious talk,' she scolded.

'Oh hell,' he replied, with a sulky bottom lip that protruded like a petulant child's.

'You have to lighten up, Gareth, I feel as if I am suffocating at times. You don't need to constantly be touching and stroking me as you do. I would for once like to watch a film all the way through without your face appearing in front of the screen.'

His whole demeanour changed to one of crestfallen adolescence. 'But you are my world,' he exclaimed. He always managed to say the right thing at the right time, she thought, but then he was a trained mouthpiece; words were his stock and trade.

'I am serious, if you can't take on board what I am saying then I am leaving.'

He now knew that she was playing hardball. 'I will make you a promise here and now that I will do my best to change to give you breathing space.' Her heart leapt, that's all she wanted, yet somehow she doubted his resolve. He was adamant that he would prove to her that he could do this thing.

It had now been a month since their heart to heart, and he had managed to restrain himself admirably, although their sexual exploits had spiced up considerably, with more visits to their purple room. She felt more relaxed around him and while he still showed affection, it was easy to deal with and not constant. They had had a lovely meal prepared by Ian and were relaxing in front of the fire; all was quiet in the house, the lads having been effectively evicted for the evening.

Gareth rose to his feet and dropped to one knee, taking out the obscenely large diamond solitaire ring that he had carried around with him for an age. 'Lisa, will you be my wife, please?' he pleaded for what seemed like the hundredth time.

'Yes, I will,' she coyly replied. Her answer totally floored him, making him feel giddy and faint.

'Really?' he replied, astonished.

'I did say yes, don't make me repeat myself!' she beamed. Slipping the ring onto her finger, beaming, he kissed her with all the passion and excitement that overflowed from every fibre of his being, lifting her from the ground and spinning her round, both now giggling like school kids.

'You have made me the happiest man on earth, and I promise you the best life ever. We have so much planning to do, when shall I arrange it for my love?' he asked tenderly.

'We have always said we love autumn.'

'Autumn it is then, sweetheart, how about early September?'

'Perfect, you choose the date. You do know that you have overlooked one thing – there is the matter of Bill Turner?' She frowned.

'Oh, I haven't, trust me. I have long awaited the chance to show that slug the door, it will be my pleasure,' he said, the menace evident in his voice as he grinned. Walking into the study, he retrieved a file and sat back down with Lisa, opening it to reveal brochures, pamphlets, seating plans, florists, details, outfitters in London, venues that held weddings on their premises. She was amazed that he seemed to have everything in place already and merely needed to set the ball in motion. They decided on Durham Castle as the venue for their nuptials. It would be a lavish affair, only the best for his one and only. There would be many guests, much to Lisa's dismay as she had hoped for a quiet wedding. They chose Ed to be their best man, with both

Davids, Bull, Mac, Steve, and Ray as ushers. All the lads from the Bull Pen would be in attendance in one role or another; security must be optimal for that day. Lisa chose her long-time friend Jackie Smales to be her maid of honour, which worked out well, as Jackie had taken a shine to Mac. Gareth had bought Lisa six tiny platinum Dragonfly hair adornments to attach to her hair, along with silk flowers encrusted with tiny crystals that glinted in the light, which would be worn down the length of tiny plaits every so often. They matched the dragonflies on the lace-covered bodice of her exquisite cream silk gown, which were covered in tiny Swarovski crystals. Gareth had bought the gownat the same time as the engagement ring he carried and had secreted it away in the wardrobe in what used to be Mac's sanctuary. Lisa left the arrangements up to Gareth, he knew her tastes inside out, yet ran his choices by her every so often to confirm he was on the right track. Including crystal encrusted cream silk slip-on court shoes that matched her dress perfectly, his eye for detail and the fact that no expense would be spared would make their day the epitome of perfection.

Lisa had gone to the farm to go through the arrangements with Jackie and to catch up on all her news. Gareth knew that she would be gone for at least two hours, ample time to issue Bill Turner with his eviction notice. He had anticipated this moment for many years. Gareth knocked on the door of Lisa's home three times before Turner answered it, the smell of sweat and oil knocking him sick as he walked past the loathsome slug of a man into the house.

'What can I do for you, Mr Edwards?' Turner inquired politely.

'I have come to give you formal notice to quit these premises with immediate effect. Lisa and I are to be married in September and she no longer wants your presence here.'

The look on Turner's face was one of total disbelief. 'This is as much my home as hers, I am going nowhere.'

'Wrong on both counts. Get your belongings packed, I will be returning tomorrow to get your key. If your fail to comply, I will remove you. Please refrain from any discussion with Lisa regarding this matter, I do not want her to be stressed in any way. Just know that this is her final word on the matter.' His instructions left no room for argument, and Turner knew by the look on Gareth's face and the tone of his voice that he would carry out his threat. When Lisa returned, Turner ignored her completely, yet this was a normal state of affairs for her; she merely wanted him out of her life for good.

In the midst of all the wedding arrangements, word came that the contender for Mac's title was ready to come to the United Kingdom to fight. Gareth was far too busy to deal with it, delegating the task of arranging the match to Bull, using the same format as before, although it was expected to be double the attendance than previously catered for due to the high rollers from the United States and Ukraine that were coming to support their boy. The amount of money changing hands that night would be obscene; admission to the club was 250 pounds per head, with the price of the very best food and drink on top. Gareth had placed a bet of half a million for Mac to win and an extra bet for Mac of 300,000, as he was not allowed to bet on himself. All the lads weighed in with their hefty bets, backing their boy all the way; after all, they often saw him in action and knew that it would take a monster to stand against his blows. The club was closed to the public that night, entirely dedicated to the aficionados of the Cage Fighting (No Rules) fraternities spanning three countries and more. Security was trebled as the obscenely wealthy arrived in their droves, pushing the club's capacity to its limits. Millions of pounds worth of muscle cars and limos arrived, making it necessary for the car park to have its own dedicated security. Mac had trained hard to slim down his legs, making him far more agile than he had ever been before without losing any power. His massive body was ripped and toned to perfection, not an ounce of body fat to be seen, and with extra coaching from Gareth he was ready to showboat his new moves. The visitors were wined and dined and as they finished their revelries the book was closed to any further wagers being placed. It was a massive pot that security took in hand that night, locking it away in the club's safe to be guarded at all times. The atmosphere built as those in attendance filed down into the basement to take the seats they had paid dearly for.

As the room settled, the contender entered the arena, and he was a monster of a man in his late thirties, standing six foot four inches, a mountain of heavy muscle – some may have said overbuilt. He sat, glaring around the room, waiting to get a glimpse of the man those in Cage Fighting circles called King Cobra. As Mac entered the arena, he assessed his opponent at a glance. He was younger and too big to dance with for too long; he needed to get this finished as quickly as possible. The tattoo of the King Cobra that adorned Mac's body had the ladies in the crowd mesmerised, its hood spread on his massive chest, the eyes shining realistically, while its body draped over his shoulder, down his back and between his legs. Mac crossed the arena in a flash, grabbing the contender and smashing his face against his knee, followed by a bone shattering kick to his ribs. The younger man's outrage was apparent, as he screamed abuse, climbing to his feet as Mac danced out of his reach. Lunging forward, his rage caused his first and last mistake, leaving himself wide open. Mac hit home with one punch, the sound of which had the crowds gasping as his opponents bottom jaw disintegrated, hanging limply from the skin that encased it, the younger man's prone body unmoving on the canvas as Mac was declared the victor and ushered out of the arena to shouts of displeasure from those who had paid to see a bloodbath, only to have witnessed a defeat with surgical precision in a few minutes. Mac's title of undefeated champion remained intact. Gareth and his lads had made a killing that night and as the crowd dispersed, he invited them all to stay for a drink, each recounting how much they had made thanks to Mac.

The wedding plans were well underway, Gareth having pulled off the ultimate coup in obtaining Ed Sheeran to sing at their wedding feast, their favourite songs being 'Perfect' and 'Thinking Out Loud'. The star had a break in his busy schedule and when Gareth offered him a king's ransom to appear the deal was sealed. There was to be a magnificent marquee with garlands of crystal encrusted silk magnolia blossoms hanging from the ceiling in their thousands, intermingled with dragonfly lights. The sides of the marquee would be lined with giant crystal-encrusted pots of honeysuckle bushes arranged to climb upwards, surrounding the guests with their heady perfume and setting the ethereal stage for their fairytale union. The ushers and groomsmen, 13 in total, were to be dressed in morning suits designed by Armani with richly embossed silken waistcoats of rampant gold and silver dragons on a midnight blue background. Two of Lisa's granddaughters were to be bridesmaids, with silk flowers woven into their long flowing locks and long A-line taffeta dresses in midnight blue to match that of the matron of honour, who was to have her hair worn up with crystal encrusted silk flowers interspersed in her hair. Gareth's waist coat would be solid gold silk embroidered with rampant red dragons. He checked the arrangements over and over again, making sure that all was to Lisa's liking. His final job was to ask one of his friends, a high court judge, to officiate in place of a justice of the peace. The stage was set, now just the honeymoon destination to be arranged. Lisa had always wanted to go to New York for Christmas, but that would mean delaying it until December; it was decided they would go to the Maldives for two weeks for their immediate honeymoon, with a second honeymoon in New York at Christmas, going the week before and coming home for a family celebration on Christmas Eve. No commercial flights needed, he would charter an executive Gulf Stream III jet to get them to their destinations, along with their security team. The guest list wasn't as extensive as first thought, Gareth being mindful of Lisa's wish for a quiet family affair; the list was merely 100 strong. He had paid as much attention to her honeymoon attire as he had to her wedding gown, especially the purple and black laced bustier with matching thong and garter belt accompanied by sheer black pure silk stockings, the whole thing covered in a sheer black gossamer silk wrap.

As the day drew steadily closer, he was careful not to renege on his promise to dial back his attentions, knowing full well that no matter how many arrangements had been made or the cost she would walk away if he backtracked. It wasn't an easy thing for him to carry off; he ached to constantly touch her, he had a real physical need to be near her, to reassure himself that she was his now and always would be. His desire to possess her body three or four times a day was a very real need that affected him to the extent of causing him pain, yet he had promised her that he would keep it to twice a day, having the effect of him upping his exercise regime, running in the early hours of silly o'clock some 15 or 20 miles a day, working out, pushing heavy weights, swimming, and pounding the treadmills in the gym until Bull could not stand the noise any longer, running and unplugging the equipment from the wall and escaping equally as quickly with his life.

Lisa constantly questioned herself; was she making the right decision? After all, a cage is still a cage, even if the bars are gold, bringing to mind the fable of the emperor and the nightingale. She needed to be able to breathe, to have a life independent from him at times, to achieve things without him. Would he allow her to be who she was? He had made her a promise, and he usually kept them, but this was the biggest ask of all; she was asking him to break his obsession.

The morning of their big day, everything went like clockwork. The hairdresser and makeup artist came to the bride's suite at the Castle, making a start on the younger members of the wedding party, little girls always being the hardest to please and keep still. Lisa had butterflies in her stomach, although her doubts were beginning to disappear as he had kept his word. As the hair and makeup was completed and everyone dressed, Lisa looked at herself in the long mirror. She hardly recognised the woman in the reflection; the heart-shaped bouquet of delicate white and purple roses, held against the exquisite cream silk gown with the fitted bodice overlaid with the finest lace of dragonflies and crystals. She marvelled as she took in every aspect of her dress, at his knack of getting everything that she adored in the right size; she could never get it right herself.

'Come on, ladies,' she beamed, 'Let's do this thing.' As she walked down the aisle towards the flower-lined bower where the officiating judge stood, the dulcet tones of Ed Sheeran singing the song Perfect rang out over the guests. Gareth, flanked by his best man, approached the bower from the front of the marquee. Arriving before Lisa, he turned to stare at the vision of perfection that was his one and only, walking towards him on Bull's arm as tears filled his eyes. This was the culmination of nearly 40 years of watching, waiting, and praying; his heart was bursting with the love that had sustained him through every heartbreaking moment that he had endured since they first met. Bull winked at Gareth as he placed Lisa's hand in his and Lisa handed her bouquet to Jackie. They faced each other as the judge began his deliberation, pausing for them to make their solemn vows.

'Lisa, you are my heart, my soul, my world. I was born to love, honour and protect you with my life. All that I am and everything I have with you I endow. You are my one, my only, we were fated to be together until the end of time.'

Her eyes welled with tears as she answered with her own vows. 'Gareth, you are my strength, the calm in my storm, the beat of my heart. The heavens fated that we be together as one until time stand still. I will honour our love and protect you with my life.'

They looked deep into each other's limpid pools, both welling with tears. Hers for the time she had wasted, and his for the relief of attaining what fate had promised at long last. The rings were bought forward on satin cushions carried by the bridesmaids as the judge continued.

'With the placing of these rings and your solemn vows I now pronounce you husband and wife. You many kiss your bride.' The place erupted with cheers and whoops from Gareth's men and the invited guests as Mr Sheeran's dulcet tones sang his song 'Thinking Out Loud', sealing the perfect day. The sumptuous wedding feast catered for vegans and meat eaters alike; champagne flowed as the guests celebrated the marriage that they had long awaited. Lisa's children, now grown with partners and families of their own, rejoiced in the knowledge that she was at last with a man that put her before all else. The maggot that was Bill Turner had packed up and left without a word, mindful of Gareth's threat, always backing down when he was faced with a man, his forte being bullying women. Gareth seized the opportunity to approach Edward, asking to speak with him in private. Leaving his wife with his three children, he followed Gareth outside.

'I have something that I need to tell you that may come as a shock.' Edward frowned, having no idea what it could be. 'I am your father, Edward,' he said, placing the laboratory findings into his hands.

The look on his face was one of astonishment and relief; then the questions came. 'How did you get a sample to test, and how long have you known?' Gareth explained the how and when of the matter to Edward's satisfaction. 'I have had to endure that pig as my father for years, why did you not come forward before? Things would have different if you had.'

Gareth agreed that had he known sooner he would have made sure he had everything he needed. He handed Edward two sets of keys. 'The first set,' he explained, 'are for the BMW 4x4 that is a present from your mother and I. The second bunch are the keys to a four bedroom detached property that is now your family home. That is my gift to you for the years that I have missed being in your life. I will furnish it to your taste – you and your wife can go shopping with your mother on our return from our honeymoon.' Edward could not take in all the revelations that Gareth had just made, so Gareth promised to sit down and talk to him at length on his return. Edward held out his hand, which his father took, and pulling him to him he hugged his son for the first time.

Returning to the marquee, he took his beloved wife by her hand and led her onto the dance floor as Michael Bolton's voice filtered through the air, regaling the guests with 'When A Man

Loves A Woman'. All watched as the couple, wrapped in each other's arms, floated across the dance floor. Gareth looked into her eyes.

'You have made me the happiest man alive, Lisa Edwards.' She kissed him deeply without saying a word as the guests joined them on the dance floor. As the record came to an end, Ed Sheeran took to the stage to play for the wedding party until the couple were ready to depart for their honeymoon. Before they left, Gareth had informed Lynette and Louise that he had gifts for them both on his return.

They excused themselves to change for their flight to the Maldives. As they came from their room, their cases had been packed and loaded into the vehicles by Bull and the grooms-men. Walking towards the front of the venue, Gareth turned to Lisa and said, 'This is my wedding present to you.' In front of her was a brand new black Maserati with a large red satin bow tied round it and the personalized number plates LYN 2. She was overwhelmed by the gift as he handed her the keys, to-tally lost for words, which was a first for Lisa. She hugged him tight. 'We have to go, my darling, as the plane has submitted its flight plan and been given clearance to take off in an hour from Teeside International Airport. Give Bull the keys and he will take your new toy home until we get back.'

The wedding guests showered them with rice and rose petals as they climbed into a black Range Rover Sports, which whisked them away followed by a second identical vehicle containing Mac, Steve, Ray, and Chris, who were to be their security detail for the two weeks of their first honeymoon. The plush cream leather interior of the Gulfstream that Gareth had chartered was filled with every possible luxury, including two bedrooms with en suite showers, a fully stocked bar and galley, plus two male stewards to take care of their every need. When all were aboard and safe-ly strapped in, the aircraft taxied down to the runway, ready to take off. This was a first for Lisa and she was terrified. Once air-borne, Gareth unbuckled her seat belt and carried her through to the master bedroom, smiling over his shoulder at the lads.

'Mrs. Edwards and I will be busy for a couple of hours. Make yourselves comfortable, lads.' The jet soared off into the late night sky, winging its way towards the Maldives carrying the happiest couple on earth at that moment, totally oblivious to what was happening half way across the world.

Sitting around a massive solid teak table in the board room in the home of Juan Montoya, former head of the Noir Valley Cartel, the attending members of the Cartel discussed the urgent matter that had been the reason for their gathering. Information had recently come into their possession regarding the assassination of two of their top cappo de regimes by an unknown assailant. At the head of the table, Montoya's grandson placed two photographs for all to see, pushing one into the centre of the table. 'This is the man who killed our brothers. It has been a long time coming, but we will have revenge for this act.' Pushing the second photograph forward, he spoke with menace. 'And this is the love of his life. I formally place a contract on behalf of the Cartel for the sum of four million US dollars. This man has to suffer, and he is no amateur, this will not be easy. I want him to watch as his love is tortured and the light fades from her eyes before he takes his last breath.' The photographs in the centre of the table were of Gareth and Lisa. All present sanctioned the hit, and as the decision was reached all that remained was to find the man to undertake the task. 'I want the top Sicario on this contract. Contact Gaviria and call in his marker; he owes me, and now is the time to collect. I want Vasques to take this one, nothing must be left to chance.' Vasques was the top Lieutenant of Escobar and later his brother Gaviria. His nickname, 'Mad Dog', filled all who heard it with fear and loathing. He openly admitted to having murdered 300 people and being involved in the murders of over 300 more. Gaviria was approached and granted Vasques leave to undertake the contract, considering his marker now paid in full. The clock was now ticking down on the two lovebirds as they flew off into the sunset to celebrate their marriage, oblivious to the fact that they had a price on their heads.

HERZ FÜR AUTOREN A HEART FOR AUTHORS À L'ÉCOUTE DES AUTEURS MIA ΚΑΡΔΙΑ ΓΙΑ ΣΥΓ
POR FORFATTARE UN CORAZÓN POR LOS AUTORES YAZARLARIMIZA GÖNÜL VERELIM SZ
PER AUTORI ET HJERTE FOR FORFATTERE EEN HART VOOR SCHRIJVERS TEMOS OS AUT
ZOÏNKERT SERCE DLA AUTORÓW EIN HERZ FÜR AUTOREN A HEART FOR AUTHORS À L'ÉCO
ÃO ВСЕЙ ДУШОЙ К АВТОРАМ ETT HJÄRTA FÖR FORFATTARE A LA ESCUCHA DE LOS AUTO
ΓΙΑ ΣΥΓΓΡΑΦΕΙΣ UN CUORE PER AUTORI ET HJERTE FOR FORFATTERE EEN
ZOÏNKERT SERCE DLA AUTORÓW EIN HERZ FÜ
ÃO ВСЕЙ ДУШОЙ К АВТОРАМ ETT HJÄRTA FÖ

The author

Julie Ann Kelly is a retired police officer from
Preston, UK. Her grand passion is the breeding
and exhibiting of Dobermanns, but she also
enjoys spending time in the beautiful Ribble
Valley countryside.
While she has previously written articles and
critiques for the Canine Press, Forever Fated is
her first novel.

The publisher

*He who stops
getting better
stops being good.*

This is the motto of novum publishing, and our focus
is on finding new manuscripts, publishing them and
offering long-term support to the authors.
Our publishing house was founded in 1997, and since
then it has become THE expert for new authors and
has won numerous awards.

**Our editorial team will peruse each manuscript
within a few weeks free of charge and without
obligation.**

You will find more information about
novum publishing and our books on the internet:

www.novum-publishing.co.uk